Sam Burnell

CHANCE IS A GAME
By Sam Burnell

Chance is a Game

Contents

INTRODUCTION 5

CHAPTER ONE 13

CHAPTER TWO 29

CHAPTER THREE 41

CHAPTER FOUR 50

CHAPTER FIVE 59

CHAPTER SIX 73

CHAPTER SEVEN 81

CHAPTER EIGHT 89

CHAPTER NINE 97

CHAPTER TEN 111

CHAPTER ELEVEN 121

CHAPTER TWELVE 130

CHAPTER THIRTEEN 136

CHAPTER FOURTEEN 142

CHAPTER FIFTEEN 154

CHAPTER SIXTEEN 165

CHAPTER SEVENTEEN 174

CHAPTER EIGHTEEN 185

CHAPTER NINETEEN	199
CHAPTER TWENTY	213
CHAPTER TWENTY-ONE	221
CHAPTER TWENTY-TWO	228
CHAPTER TWENTY-THREE	241
CHAPTER TWENTY-FOUR	250

CHANCE IS A GAME

by Sam Burnell

•

First published in eBook and paperback 2023

•

© Sam Burnell 2023

•

The right of Sam Burnell to be identified as the author of this work has been asserted by her in accordance with the Copyright, Designs and Patents Act 1988.

All rights reserved. No part of this publication may be reproduced, stored in or introduced into a retrieval system, or transmitted, in any form, or by any means (electronic, mechanical, photocopying, recording or otherwise) without the prior written permission of the writer. Any person who does any unauthorised act in relation to this publication may be liable to criminal prosecution and civil claims for damages.

Thank you for respecting the hard work of this author.

INTRODUCTION

London – Spring 1553

Habit might have been his undoing.

Davyd Garstang, neat, well dressed in solid brown well-woven wool, had a routine that never varied. It often made him wonder that the precision needed as part of his trade produced something that gave men such a disorganised mind. It seemed a world of opposites; it was a question he often pondered.

Garstang controlled the Tinwell brewery attached by one wall to the Bird in Hand Tavern, and behind it, trickling and sluicing its way towards the Thames, was Mutton Brook, supplying the water that would become beer. He had worked here for five years, the process had been improved, three more vats had been added, the Tinwell brewery was among the largest in London, and Garstang was proud of his achievement. It was, after all, one that paid him well. He checked the brewery alone at the end of the week to ensure everything was in order. It gave him a certain peace of mind.

Brewing was one of his master's more legitimate businesses. Time overseas had taught him to recognise the value of hops. Many didn't like the bitter taste it gave to the brew, but the simple fact was it lasted longer and could be stored. Beer brewed by the alewives lasted no more than a few days, so the process was as tedious and never-ending as baking bread. But hops had changed that. And whether London liked it or not, it didn't matter; the new bitter taste was all that was served in Devereux's taverns, and no one was going elsewhere.

Clean brown boots crunched on the gravel before the locked door. Garstang hitched his cloak over his shoulder, revealing a broad ring of keys hooked over his belt. Selecting one, he slotted it into the lock. Well used and on thick leather hinges recessed into the stonework, the door, released from the lock, swung silently inwards. Hooking the ring back on his belt and stepping inside, Garstang closed the door behind him, pulling the cloak back from his shoulder and shaking the fabric back into place; his eyes surveyed his brewery. He'd carry a lamp during the winter months, but lighter evenings lit the interior from high windows set into the stonework. Shutters were held back by iron hooks resting in loops; they were only closed when the weather was bad enough to force rain inside, and then only those where the water was worst. A brewery needed to breathe, the stale air from the fermentation vats needed to escape; otherwise, it stole a man's senses, sending him into the sleep of the dead.

The scent inside the stone walls was one he knew well. Rich, heady, thick and pleasing. It eradicated the stench of the city at any time of year, even in the putrid summer months. When the sun was upon London, Garstang found the brewery a relief. The midden at the end of the muddy street where the Bird in Hand sat stunk in the heat. The wretched mire stopped reeking only when winter placed a solid ice crust over the top, sealing in the aroma of waste. It was the curse of the brewer to have a sensitive nose, he supposed, and he objected to having his infused with the scent of filth.

At the top of the building was a neat row of open windows. They allowed light into the inside of the brewhouse, but more importantly, let out the fumes. During the summer, shafts of bright sunlight ran at angles across the building, the ever-present dust seemingly trapped inside these narrow corridors of light. In the winter, it was a different kind of light, grey and cold like river water, flowing into the brewery and bringing little warmth.

"Jake? Where are you, boy?" Garstang called, casting his eyes around the still interior. Jake worked on the malting floor, continually turning the grains. He slept in the brewhouse, waking twice a night to rake the barley.

"Boy? Come here now." Garstang's voice was a little louder. Nothing moved in the shadowy interior. "Jake?"

No reply.

Where had that idiot boy got to?

Garstang stopped at the malting floor, picking up Jake's rake. He pulled it through the grains and cursed. It was the boy's job to ensure the grains were turned so the emerging shoots didn't knit together, and the rake prongs, filled with a thatch of new roots, told him the centre of the malting floor was a solid mat. He dropped the rake into several other areas on the floor and cursed again.

All the same.

These hadn't been turned for at least a day, maybe a little longer. The whole lot on the malting floor was ruined. Once they wound themselves together, it was impossible to separate them. When he found Jake, the boy was in for a beating. The whole floor needed to be cleared, and the process begun again. The grains on the malting floor would be turned and raked for two weeks. These had been here for under a week, so a whole week of production would be lost. And Myles Devereux was an impatient master.

Garstang flung the rake back against the wall; the wood shaft rattled noisily on the stonework. Devereux would not be happy when he discovered that production would drop in about a week when there wasn't enough mash. The boy was going to suffer for this! Devereux didn't understand or didn't want to understand brewing. He'd not appreciate that if there wasn't enough mash, then ale production would fall. He would just tell Garstang to work harder and make up the shortfall, and that wasn't how it worked. The only saving grace was that the problem wouldn't be noticed for almost two weeks.

Garstang tugged his short, dark beard as he considered the problem. He could hide the loss, hold back an amount from the previous week and count it towards the short week. It might work. He'd have to think about it. If he also used the following week's production, he could smooth the figures out and use the total from the three weeks evenly. All three weeks would be down, but fluctuations did happen, and it would mean the sudden drop when the grains had been ruined at least wouldn't be noticed - hopefully.

Garstang grumbled as he walked across the brewery floor. Why was he bothering to delude himself? Devereux wouldn't be fooled. He'd notice the drop and immediately call Garstang to account for it. It would not be a moment to look forward to. Blaming Jake would get him nowhere. He knew that the fault would be his to bear. If he smoothed it over three weeks, it might reduce his punishment to just an ear scalding, and he could try and placate Devereux with a future promise of an increase in production as well. He would have to give this some very careful thought. If he offered Devereux more, he'd expect Garstang to deliver that amount every week.

Garstang continued with his circuit of the lower floor, no longer in a good mood, and thankfully, nothing else seemed amiss. None of the brewing vats were leaking, the floor was swept clean, and grain sacks were stored correctly. But from somewhere he could hear a splashing sound. Frowning, Garstang made his way towards the middle of the building. Mutton brook was diverted, running in a stone channel through the centre of the brewery before exiting and continuing its course towards the river.

On its journey, it provided the citizens of London with drinking water for animals. A dye shop in End Street relied upon it, and often, the water was tinted blue or green after this before it joined Church Brook and doubled in size. Then, carrying the filth from the streets, it made its way to join the river. The water was running silently; when there had been heavy rains, it could flood over the floor and, in its haste, escape from the channel to splash the stone flags on the brewery floor. But not today, and there hadn't been any significant rain for weeks. Puzzled, Garstang stooped to observe the water level in the channel. It was low.

The noise came again; he was sure it was above him this time. Level with the top of the wooden brewing vats was a mezzanine reached by a ladder. He didn't usually go up it at night if all seemed well. The vats would bubble if the fermentation process was too vigorous, but this noise sounded too irregular. What had the lads done now?

Cursing under his breath, Garstang set his feet onto the ladder's rungs. This took him to the wooden boards that ran along the side of the wall behind the brewing vats. It was dark. The light from the rows of windows missed the planking, illuminating the centre of the brewhouse and leaving the rest in a dark shadow.

Garstang stepped onto the wooden boards, rubbing his hands together to remove the barley dust they had gathered during the climb, when he heard a metallic clanking.

Garstang frowned. "Jake?"

There was no reply.

The noise came to him again from the far corner. It sounded like iron links, heavy and clanking against one another. The sound erratic.

"Jake, get your arse here now. I know what you've done, and there'll be a tanning for your hide, so don't make it bloody worse by hiding in the corner," Garstang threatened, his hands balled into fists resting on his hips.

No reply.

"Jake! I'm warning you," Garstang said again and then demanded. "Get here, now!"

There was the slightest noise from an iron link shifting on another. A single metallic clink

Then silence.

"Jake?" A sudden and irrational sense of unease crawled, spider-like, up Garstang's back.

"I don't think Jake can hear you." A voice, little more than a whisper, replied.

Garstang stepped backwards hurriedly.

The links loosened and suddenly ran free, clattering to the wooden boards.

Garstang, a cry for help trapped in his constricted throat, turned and flung himself towards the ladder. His cloak didn't move as quickly as he did, and a length of heavy wool caught around his right leg, trapping it momentarily. Garstang plunged forward, his balance lost, hands outstretched. He landed hard, sliding towards the ladders, his palms collecting splinters before he stopped.

"Let me help you up," a voice reeking of evil intent said from behind him.

Scrabbling onto his knees, Garstang began to shuffle towards the ladder until his escape was stopped, the material of his doublet tightening around his neck. He could feel a powerful fist fastened into the cloth on his back. Choking, Garstang found himself hauled to his feet, his fingers feebly trying to pull the collar from his neck.

"Please ...." It was a thought only. The sound wouldn't emerge from his throat.

The pressure on his windpipe slackened for the briefest moment, long enough for his lungs to pull in his last gasped breath. Around his neck, cold, rough and heavy, the chain tightened. With his hands on the links, he tried to pull at the iron that was digging deep into the flesh of his neck.

"Please ... please ...." The silent plea bounced around the inside of his mind that darkened with every silent word.

A childlike gurgle of laughter filled with pleasure was close to his right ear. It was the last noise Garstang heard. The sound after that was two solid thumps, the first his body hitting the boards and the second something solid slamming into the back of his head.

CHAPTER ONE

London – Three Weeks Ago

If a man mentioned the White Hart tavern, it was enough to raise an eyebrow amongst his fellows, known as it was for supplying a lot more than ale and middling fayre. If he wanted to borrow money, sell something that he had chanced upon, find a man, strike a deal without the risk of being overheard or find men to do tasks he'd rather not carry out himself, then the White Hart was the choice of tavern.

The building itself was old, built a score of years before Old King Hal had been born. It was sturdy, oak timbered with thick, well-kept daub walls, solid-fitting shutters and even several leaded windows on the top floor. It was not amongst London's more stylish inns, comprised as it was of a series of extensions around the original building, constructed very much with purpose and not elegance in mind, but it was amongst her larger. The yard at the rear was big enough to host various entertainments, and the high walls also provided a secure marketplace where transactions could not be overheard. Amongst the buildings at the back was a Smith's workshop, a bakery, stabling for thirty horses and accommodation for Devereux's men. Its size made it the natural centre of Myles Devereux's businesses.

Devereux, with his vague noble lineage, styled himself as being among London's elite, despite his taverns and pawn shops being frequented by the poor. He allegedly had family connections to the Earl of Devon through a distant cousin, a Plantagenet with a tenuous claim to the English throne. Myles styled himself as nobility, dressed better than many of the queen's courtiers, and probably possessed more gold than some of them. Myles' court was not, however, in a royal palace. It was at the White Hart, and it was a very different kind of court from the queen's.

The tap room was rarely empty. Four of Devereux's men were always present to ensure ale was paid for and order kept and that those wishing to see their master were made known to Matthew, Devereux's capable lieutenant.

Matthew was in charge of Devereux's men, ensuring the security of his master, the White Hart and the rest of Myles Devereux's properties. His bald head was topped with a dark red leather bonnet; beneath that a thickly muscled neck led down to broad shoulders and a torso encased in a leather jacket with a row of polished buckles up the front. He was always armed outside the White Hart when there would be a sword belt strapped to his waist; when he was inside, there was a broad knife neatly fitted into a scabbard on his belt and another, shorter, nestling in a wrist guard. At first glance, he could be taken for a soldier, and rumour indeed regularly mentioned that he had been part of the royal guard at some point, but now he worked solely for Devereux.

The main tavern room was open, the ceiling held up by a dozen rough, blackened oak pillars that bore the weight of the upper floor. Between them was scattered a disorderly arrangement of unmatched stools and benches; the floor, covered in a thick layer of rushes, was cleared monthly. The whole lot barrowed out and used for bedding in the stables, but only after several of Devereux's rat boys had scavenged through it for anything that had been dropped in the mire.

Not stupid enough to keep their finds, the filthy children presented their prizes to Matthew. Buttons, broken buckles, leather straps and the occasional coin were exchanged for food and the right to sleep on the tavern floor. Matthew had been known to part with a groat if anything of significance were ever unearthed. The boys with lively eyes and empty stomachs saw everything that went on in the White Hart, and were one of their master's reliable sources of information.

It was Friday.

Myles Devereux's favourite day of the week, opportunities, new business and affirmation of whether the week had been good were all revealed on Friday. His debtors called to pay their dues or take out more loans, his accounts were completed for the week, the coins tallied to the ledger, and the weeks' worth was totalled. New business deals were struck, and occasionally, news reached Myles that he could profit from. Myles Devereux's collection of businesses, from the taverns to his money lending, might be morally questionable, but they were undeniably profitable.

Myles liked Fridays. Perhaps not as much as he once had. Some months ago, his bookkeeper had been murdered, and the news had been brought to him on a Friday. It had been the beginning of a chain of events that had very nearly cost him his life, and the shadow of it dampened some of his childish excitement about the day.

His clerk, Peter, was already in the room outside his own. Debtors were sent up the stairs and admitted by Matthew, and under his watchful gaze, debts were paid, and amounts were entered in the ledger. His last bookkeeper had not only had the effrontery to get himself murdered, but after his death, Myles had found that the man had been systematically stealing from him for a year. So now, a very close watch was kept on both the money and the ledgers. In one respect, it had worked out well; the murdered man had been paid eight pounds a year as his bookkeeper, and he had not been replaced. Instead, Myles used his clerk, Peter Smythe, paying him only two pounds. A saving of six pounds, and it went some way to alleviating the pain he felt from the theft.

The lad was quick-witted, and once he had got over his initial nerves of working directly under the supervision of Matthew and Devereux, he had proven himself. His writing was faultless and neat. Initially, Myles had completed the columns requiring arithmetic, but it soon became apparent that Peter was quite capable of calculating the balances, and Myles now just checked them. The boy was very well-paid and eager to prove his worth.

There were two rooms upstairs in the White Hart, an outer room where Devereux conducted his business. It was Spartan in terms of furnishing: a table for his clerk to sit at, two chairs, a coffer against one wall, and a small table flanked another. A door that had once been in a church and had opened to a vestry now separated the outer room from Myles' own. Sometimes, it would stand ajar so the opulence could be seen, but mostly, it was solidly closed. It was rarely locked, but should the need arise, a keyhole led to an operational heavy lock that sealed the door to the frame. Once the key had turned, it would be easier to access Myles' room via the daub and timber walls on either side than mount an assault on the four inches of oak filling the door frame.

Today, the door to Myles' room was closed; those who came were denied a glimpse of Devereux's private luxury.

The only opulence in the room today was Myles, dressed as he was in his tailor's latest creation. Even he was having difficulty keeping his eyes from the sleeves of his doublet, and Myles was satisfied that everyone who had seen him today had not missed them either. The sleeves, made from a thick black velvet, were slashed, the openings leaf-shaped, and the edges of each were ornamented with pearls, as white and glowing as a summer moon. Devereux had provided the pearls to his tailor, Master Drew, after they came to him in settlement of a debt. Myles doubted they had belonged to the owner, and rather than attempting to resell them as ladies' jewels, he had decided to decorate himself with them instead, much to Matthew's annoyance.

The contrast between the saturnine black and the white natural elegance was heightened by a deep purple silk that showed through the slashes. The colour was banned from all but royalty, but Devereux's tailor had skillfully created the colour by layering two fine transparent silks. A rich, deep blue covered a blood-red fabric, and the result was undeniably and satisfyingly purple. Master Drew had been a little nervous about involving himself in such a breach of the sumptuary statutes. Myles' argument that the law referred only to dyed purple silk and he was not asking for clothes cut from such cloth, plus a payment in gold, had allowed Drew to forget his qualms about the legality of the clothing.

This Friday was proving to be better than usual. It was the first quarter day of the year; Devereux had a dozen men who paid him four times a year, all of whom had dutifully presented themselves and their money. There had been a full turnout of his weekly debtors to hand over their dues. Plus, Barnaby Denton, wheelwright, had taken out a large loan to buy land for stabling, and Devereux's lawyer was assigning it to him until the debt was paid, the legal fee being added to Denton's debt. Cubby Harper had paid his debt off and foolishly taken another loan. Myles was in a good mood. The business of the day was almost concluded.

Leggy Dodds, who had been waiting in the tap room of the White Hart for his turn to see Devereux, was summoned up the stairs to Myles' presence. Leggy, agile, spare-framed and with a face that never seemed at rest, worked for Devereux, running cockfights at his various taverns during the week. He had a skill with birds; he could find unlikely-looking winning fowl and possessed a talent for whipping a crowd into a betting frenzy. His trade was proclaimed by the leather jerkin he wore, decorated with feathers from the tails of the winners bound into thin strips of leather and hanging in tassels from his shoulders, and on his head, a floppy felt hat decorated with brown and white cock feathers. Leggy's only problem was that the curse of his profession meant he too had a gambling habit, and it wasn't birds; it was dice. So, he supplemented his wages from Devereux by working on the docks; Devereux knew but chose to ignore it as long as Leggy remained a proficient cock-master in the evenings.

Matthew admitted Leggy to the room. Leggy held before him a sack of rough hessian bundled in his arms.

"I've sommat to sell, sir," Leggy announced smiling, his brows disappearing under the rim of his bonnet; he proudly thrust the ball of rags towards Myles.

With a look of distaste, Myles took a step backwards. "If that's a feral bird in there, you can take it away."

"It's nah bird, sir," Leggy announced, grinning, his nose twitching as he did.

"Well, whatever it is, put it on there," Myles waved his hand towards the table.

Leggy reverently placed his burden on the wood top and flipped the filthy cloth away with the practised hand of a showman. Inside was no squawking bantam but a box. Intricate marquetry, spliced with mother of pearl, a rich tapestry of chestnut wood and shimmering pink and silver shell. With a flourish of his arm, Leggy stepped back, his feathered strings swinging in the air.

Myles stared between the wooden cube mosaic and Leggy. "And?"

Leggy, looking slightly crestfallen, his mouth sinking towards his chin for a moment, said, "It's a treasure, sir. Craftsmanship like that has to be worth summat."

Myles stepped towards the box, circling the table on which it sat. The top was decorated with a multi-pointed star, and running diagonally across it was an arrow, the fletching picked out in gold. Myles turned it slowly. Each side was the same, a geometric pattern repeating around the box. Picking it up, he was immediately surprised by the weight. He lifted it to examine the bottom, and nothing inside shifted. No coins slid. There was no tell-tale rattle to hint at the contents. The sides were perfect, and if the lid lifted, there was no indication of where the top separated from the bottom.

Myles set the box down and stepped backwards, folding his arms. "Does it open?"

Leggy shrugged. "I dunno, sir, there's nowhere to put a key."

Myles turned the box again, slowly casting his eyes over each side. A marquetry diamond had the slightest variance, a darker line around its edge marking it out from the rest of the pattern. Myles held the box down with his left hand and pressed the diamond. The box emitted a satisfying click, and he felt the lid shift beneath his palm when the catch was released; Myles raised it. Matthew and Leggy, opposite him, both stepped forward. Myles closed the lid quickly, preventing them from viewing the interior.

"Empty," Myles announced bluntly. "A groat."

"What! A groat, fer that? It's worth more, sir," Leggy blurted, his eyes popping from their sockets and his mouth open, revealing a row of chipped front teeth.

"I am sure it is, and I would imagine its owner did indeed pay more, but as pleasing as it may look, Leggy, it's very distinctive and stolen. It's not a plate that can be melted and reformed. There really isn't much I can do with it, is there?" Myles explained, his tone impatient, his words clipped.

Leggy's face was a study in disappointment. "But you could put it in one of yer shops, sir."

Myles let out a long breath, his dark eyes fixed on those of the cock-master. "You brought this to me because it's stolen; no one would believe you have the right to sell this, and if you are caught with it, you'll have difficulty pulling birds from bags with only one hand. If you can't openly sell it, how do you expect me to?"

"I suppose .... but it's a nice box," Leggy pointed, unwilling to give up on his recent acquisition.

Myles didn't give Leggy another moment to change his mind. "Matthew, give Leggy a groat and send him to the taproom if you will."

Matthew held out the coin in a gloved hand. Leggy took it and, as was his habit, ran it across a nail that was tied to his belt.

Matthew raised a hand, and Leggy ducked. "Out of here, you impudent, cur. How dare you check one of Master Devereux's coins?"

"Sorry, habit, sir," Leggy said, scuttling towards the door at speed.

"Go on," Matthew took two quick steps towards the man, chasing him from the room, and then his eyes rested on the filthy rags Leggy had left on the table. Scooping them up, he hauled the door to the stairs open, throwing the rags after Leggy. "And take that stinking pile with you as well."

Matthew closed the door with more force than was necessary and, shaking his head, turned towards Myles. "He's a cheeky shit. He should have been bloody grateful for a groat. If you ask me, it's more than it's worth. As you said, there's little you can do with it."

Myles, ignoring him, picked up the box from the table and stalked towards his room.

Matthew rolled his eyes, "Have you forgotten? You've still got Finch waiting to see you.

Myles groaned. He had forgotten that there was the final issue of the day to deal with.

Marcus Finch.

Finch had been waiting in the tap room of the White Hart and purposefully left until last. He'd been summoned early, and everyone who had been to the tavern would have seen him waiting – and wondered. Soon enough, they'd find out why he'd been there.

"Get Finch up here," Myles said, annoyed. Not because he was concerned about the coming confrontation or its impact on his business but because he had better things to do. The box was calling to him, and he wanted to explore the contents, not deal with a fool who thought he could outwit Myles Devereux.

Finch arrived, his wool cap held before him in both hands, his hooked nose sitting beak-like over the thatched nest of his untidy beard. Finch's restless eyes roving the room had noted that only Myles and Matthew were present; the clerk had gone, and none of Devereux's men were present – so it would be a very private conversation. If the prolonged wait had made him nervous, his situation now served only to worsen his condition, and Finch's sallow complexion paled.

Myles folded his arms and stared at the man. "If I look unhappy, Finch, it's because you are now a bloody inconvenience as well as a thief."

Finch's eyes widened in fright. "Sorry, master …. I."

"I've better things to do, Finch, than discuss your errors. We both know you are guilty. So kindly confess, and we can move this matter to a swifter close," Myles said bluntly, his right hand smoothing a crease in a velvet sleeve.

"Guilty, sir, I don't know what you mean?" Finch stammered, twisting the hat harder in his sweaty hands.

Myles' eyes found the ceiling, and he cursed silently. "Don't make this worse by lengthening this interview."

Finch switched his gaze to Matthew. "I am sorry, I really don't understand, sir."

The man's appeal to Matthew was wasted; he returned Finch's gaze with a hard stare. "You'd be well advised, Finch, to tell Master Devereux the truth."

Finch took a hesitant step backwards, the hat clutched defensively to his chest.

"Right, I've had enough. Finch, you've had your chance. Get Herbert up here, now," Myles said, exploding in sudden movement from the wall he had been resting against and sending Finch back two more paces.

Matthew hauled the door open at the top of the stairs and bellowed. "Herbert. Up here now."

The sound of heavy footfalls as a man bounded up the stairs two at a time followed.

Finch's mouth fell open as he saw Herbert stepping through the door. "You ...."

"Yes, indeed, Finch .... I gave you a chance, an opportunity to grasp at the fateful straws of redemption, but instead, you've used them as kindling, and my temper is now fully aflame," Myles pronounced. "Tell me how you could ever think that you," Myles waved his hand towards Finch, "could best me?"

Finch swallowed. His eyes were wide with fear, and the skin beneath the stubble had paled to the colour of milk.

"Silence, Finch, is not a defence?" Myles said, his hands behind his back as he sauntered slowly across the room.

"You see, Finch, it was simply a matter that the numbers did not balance. I was supplying the Unicorn with around ten barrels of beer a week, and the takings collected by Matthew were telling me that you'd only sold eight. Perhaps a barrel was breached? It happens occasionally; a drayman drops one, or a barrel stave gives way, but that's one barrel, an occasional, not even annual, occurrence. And you, Finch, have been short of two barrels for just over six weeks," Myles stopped before Finch and glared at him. "So, who did you sell it to? Who have you been profiting from?"

"We did lose a few barrels like you said, Master Devereux ...." Finch tried, his voice little more than a squeak.

"No, you didn't. This is Herbert. You know him as Hardwood, and he bought a barrel from you yesterday. Shame he works for me," Myles said, his voice cold and edged with ice.

Finch's eyes darted between the grinning Herbert and Myles, the untidy, coarse brown beard trembling on his chin.

"Exactly right, Master Finch. You are in a place where you would rather not be and with little hope of extracting yourself," Myles said bluntly. "Who did you sell the other barrels to?"

"It weren't my fault .... Really it weren't .... I were forced to, Master Devereux, I swear by the Grace of God." Finch began to plead, the cap in his hands screwed up to a quarter of its original size.

"I care not for God's grace, and I doubt very much if the almighty wishes to be tarnished with your sins either. Who did you sell it to?" Myles demanded.

Finch remained silent.

Matthew's gloved hand hit Finch around the back of the head, making the man yelp and stagger across the room.

"Tell Master Devereux," Matthew said before delivering another persuasive blow to the back of his head.

"Please, Master, I had no choice...."

Another blow.

"It were Bennett, I sold it to Bennett," Finch cried, his arms wrapped around his head to protect himself.

"Bennett?" Myles growled, his eyes widening in disbelief. Bennett was Devereux's rival in London, and no one who worked for him would be foolish enough to deal with him, or so he had thought.

"Aye, sir, we had spare; he had a need, and I sold 'im it. I pass the money to you," Finch bleated, his hands still around his head, the ugly beard jutting between them.

"I'm no fool, Finch. The takings from the Unicorn account for eight barrels for the last six weeks, not ten. Even if you sold him the two at a lower price, you didn't pass that money to Matthew, did you?" Myles said.

"I was gunna, I were just waiting to 'im to pay," Finch squawked, the felt hat in his hands patched with sweat.

"Are you trying to tell Master Devereux you gave Bennett twelve barrels of his beer without taking any money from him? How foolish do you think he is?" Matthew said, turning to Herbert, who was enjoying the show immensely and asked. "And did you pay Finch for the barrel you bought?"

"Aye, sir, I did. Wi' the marked coin you gave me," Herbert's grin broadened.

"And when was this?" Myles asked, a degree of calm returning to his voice.

"Yesterday, sir," Herbert replied.

"So why, Finch, was that coin not included in the takings Matthew collected this morning?" Myles asked, one eyebrow raised in enquiry.

"Err, it coulda been swapped, given in change. I might have passed it on," Finch tried.

"Oh, come on, Finch, he paid you with an Angel. You don't give those away in change. You ran the Unicorn. It's not the royal court. Your patrons rarely have more than a groat in their pockets," Myles said, flinging his arms wide.

"I might ha' forgotten to include it," Finch tried again with another pointless defence.

"I've had enough. Firstly, you sold my beer to Bennett, of all people. You've kept the money from this, and you honestly believed your theft would not be noticed," Myles stated, pointing a long finger toward Finch.

"Please, master," Finch pleaded, lurching forward, his arms outstretched as he dropped to his knees. As he descended the edge of the cap, he was still clutching brushed Myles' sleeve, and one of the pearls, snagged by the wool threads, was torn from its fixing. The iridescent sphere fell between them. Finch, already on his knees, dived towards it, slapping a hand on the floor to capture it; he succeeded only in hastening the pearl's passage across the floor. All three men watched as it rolled slowly towards a gap in the planked floor. It teetered on the edge, looked for a second as if it might roll back, then changing its mind, it dropped silently from sight.

There was a moment of silence.

Myles stepped back, his hand clutching his injured sleeve, a look of pure loathing directed towards Finch. Matthew had his hand wound in the material at the back of Finch's neck and hauled the man to his feet.

"Sir, I am sorry ...." Finch's words were cut off as the material around his neck choked his throat.

"Get him out of my sight!" Myles growled, eyes alight with fury.

Matthew hauled the door open and ejected Finch; as he exited the door, a boot in the small of his back sent him sprawling down the stairs head first, wailing as he landed on the steps, his arms flung out before him. Matthew followed him down at a slower pace.

Herbert was still in the room, his eyes wide, his expression a mixture of fear and delight. The noise of Finch arriving painfully at the foot of the stairs could be heard outside the room.

"Want to join him?" Myles asked his mouth a hard line, eyes fixed unwaveringly on Herbert.

"No, master ...." Herbert stammered.

"Find Matthew after he's finished with Finch; the Unicorn needs a new landlord. Now, get out," Myles said, turning towards the door to his room.

"Sir, thank you, sir," Herbert said, a look of delighted sudden surprise on his face.

"Leave."

"Yes, sir. You can rely on me, Master Devereux, thank you ...."

"*OUT NOW*," Myles's voice, like a thrust of steel, had Herbert backing towards the door, still rattling words of thanks as he went.

Myles closed the door to his room and leaned his back against it. Finch had given him a headache. He'd been dealing with Bennett, Myle's rival in London. That was something he hadn't bargained on. He'd assumed the man had supplied the ale to one of the few independent taverns or even to one of the guilds or a large house within the city, but not to Bennett. He'd find out more, he had no doubt, when Matthew returned.

His eyes travelled toward the snapped threads on his sleeve, and he cursed Finch.

CHAPTER TWO

Matthew sent Finch into the welcoming, if not too gentle, embrace of two of his men at the bottom of the stairs. He'd deal with him later.

Rogan, one of the rat boys, was waiting for him patiently, a wooden cup in his hands, clasping it like a chalice. Matthew walked towards him and held his hand out. Taking the cup, he tipped the contents into a gloved palm and inspected the offerings. Very little. Three unmatched bone buttons, a bronze buckle missing the clasp, the bowl from a pewter spoon, a dozen clothes pins and a chipped bone dice.

Matthew poured them back into the cup. "Poor findings this week."

"Aye, master. We always looks as best we can," Rogan replied, sounding equally disappointed.

"I'm sure you do. None of the other lads are cheating on you, are they?" Matthew asked, meeting the boy's eyes below a scraggy fringe of hair; the rest of his head was encased in a leather cap, too big for him, the side flaps hanging down to his shoulders.

The boy shook his head vigorously, the sides of his headgear flapping like a hound's ears. "They wouldn't dare, master."

"Good. Take this to Farrell." Matthew replaced the offerings and handed the cup back. Farrell ran one of Devereux's poorer pawn shops. The bronze and pewter would go into a bucket for melting down, and the buttons and pins would be matched with others and sold as sets. Very little went to waste. The rushes were used as bedding in the stables, and then, soiled with muck, they would be forked into a wagon and taken to the fields. More work for the rat boys.

Sometimes, Matthew would drop a coin he had marked onto the White Hart's floor just before the rushes were removed. It was this that helped ensure the boys' honesty. If that coin were not in the cup Rogan presented to Matthew, there would be the Devil to pay. All of the boys would be evicted from sleeping in the tavern, and they'd be forced to forage for their own food. It had happened twice before, and the culprit had never been seen again on both occasions. Sanctuary and food were too valuable. The boys might be prey to a cuff round the head or a boot up the arse from Matthew or his men, but on the whole, sleeping in the Hart was akin to being in a fortress, and it leant a degree of safety to their lives they would not find elsewhere.

Matthew returned; he found Myles had abandoned the outer room and was seated at his desk. The window behind him was open, the shutters wide on a cold London, the chilled air pressed back by the orange blaze in the hearth. Matthew thought it a waste of firewood, but he never said so. His footfalls were softened by the rugs spread across the boards, and the warmth from the fire was retained by walls that were blanketed in tapestries. Set in the room was a four-poster bed that Devereux had taken as part of a payment for a debt and had refused to part with. The room was not one you would expect to find above a tavern like the White Hart, but then the man who lived in it wasn't one you'd expect to find there either.

"What have you done with Finch?" Myles asked.

"Nothing .... yet," Matthew replied.

"Hmmm, it's a little difficult after recent events to have him turn up floating in the river," Myles said, annoyed.

"Agreed. Finch has stolen from you. Why not hand him to Justice Daytrew to deal with?" Matthew suggested.

"What! And have the rest of London know the shit robbed me!" Myles exploded. "I'll not be a victim and a fool."

"What do you want me to do with him then? If I send him from London, he's just as likely to turn back up, and that's just as bad. Word will get out. It always does, especially when Bennett is involved. You can't leave him unpunished," Matthew said.

"I've no intention of doing that. Lock him up here for a few weeks, and then we can get rid of Finch," Myles said bluntly.

"It's not safe. You need to put more time between recent events and another body turning up," Matthew advised.

"Make sure it doesn't. Isn't that the obvious answer?" Myles snapped back.

"Questions are still going to be asked if he disappears," Matthew said, then an evil smile spread across his lips, "Send him to Jeriah; tell him you've sent him a new assistant."

Myles laughed. "Christ, we were well rid of Jeriah; he's the Devil's man if any ever was."

"And he is happy in hell, I have no doubt," Matthew replied, "If you deliver Finch to him, I doubt he'll be a problem for long."

Jeriah had worked for Devereux, albeit briefly. He took a delight in violence, and worse, he liked to keep trophies from his victims. A string of fingers had hung from his belt, and when one of those belonged to a parish elder, Myles had to admit enough was enough. Devereux had a contract to dispose of the dead from the Tower and passed Jeriah sideways to work in the prison. The man had been foolishly delighted by the appointment, which removed him from among the ranks of Devereux's men, who were increasingly nervous around him. Rumour had it he had moved away from fingers and had begun a collection of ears in his new post.

"It's not quite final enough, though, is it?" Myles said, not completely happy with the proposal.

"He'll be under lock and key. What do you think his chances are of escaping from the Tower? Even the goaler and his men are not free to come and go as they choose. They are as much prisoners in there as those poor bastards chained in the dungeons. If you send Finch to Jeriah, you know where he'll be, and he'll suffer for his crimes; Jeriah will not be an easy master to please," Matthew said.

"Alright. Next time you collect the dead from the Tower, give Jeriah a groat, tell him Finch is a gift from me," Myles conceded, still feeling he was letting Finch off too lightly for his crimes. "Just keep him locked up until you next go."

Collecting the bodies from the Tower was Devereux's only way into and out of the fortress. His men, along with a cart, arrived every week and took away the deceased from the prison. Matthew would include Finch next time they went, and he had an arrangement with the keeper who wouldn't turn down an offer of free labour. And Finch would not re-emerge with the cart rumbled back through the gates.

Myles' fingers had strayed back to the box again. "Poor bastard. How long do you think he'll have his ears?"

"Who cares. Jeriah will not keep his temper for long, and then Finch's demise will have nothing to do with you," Matthew replied, laughing.

"It's not empty, Matthew," Myles said. Finch had already been forgotten about, and his mind turned back to the much more interesting prize Leggy Dodds had brought him.

Matthew stepped towards it, and Myles lifted the lid and turned the box towards the other man, exposing an intricate gold mechanism to the light. It nestled neatly inside the box, which was velvet-lined and padded to keep it secure. The top was gold; it appeared to be made of a disc in the middle with two more wheels surrounding it; around them were engraved symbols neither man had ever seen before.

"What the ...." Matthew said, gawping at the gold instrument.

"I have no idea," Myles said, wrapping his fingers around the edges of the top of the object, he began to prise it from the box. Once free of the velvet, a tiny key on a delicate chain was revealed, inset into the velvet padding.

The sides of the object were, to a degree, open. Sheets of gold cut through with a series of diamond-shaped windows allowed the viewer to see inside. Myles turned it on its side and stared into the packed interior. Metal wires, wound and spooled, wheels of different sizes held apart by bronze spacers, and a delicate chain with flat links ran around the outside of some of the larger wheels.

Myles prodded a small lever on the side of a metallic box with his forefinger. A cog, its edge exposed from the right side of the box, turned; the mechanism inside clicked, and the flat disc on the top rotated slightly.

"Do you know what it is?" Matthew asked, dropping into a seat opposite Myles.

Myles shook his head, his eyes still fixed on the treasure. "Not a clue."

Turning the box back, he inserted the small gold key into a hole and turned it; the mechanism clicked as he did. "Look, the loop here disappears as I turn this."

"I can see that," Matthew said, "But what do all those markings on the top mean?"

Myles removed the key and put the box down. The top surface comprised large wheels, one inside another, three in total. On them were engraved symbols unlike any Myles had ever seen before. When the lever on the side was pressed again, the mechanism clicked, and all three wheels moved in opposite directions.

"That's Jewish, I'm sure of it. Maya would be able to tell you," Matthew said, pointing at the script.

"You think I am going to show this to Maya? That," Myles said, pointing towards the golden box, "is bloody dangerous. Can you imagine what the Catholic fathers would make of it?"

Matthew laughed. "The work o' the Devil, for sure."

Myles picked it up, turning it this way and that.

"Is it all gold?" Matthew asked, swiping his bonnet from his head and discarding it on the desk.

Myles shook his head. "The top is, the workings I don't think are."

"I say we melt it down and take our profit from the gold," Matthew planted his elbows on the table and leaned towards the box.

Myles regarded him with a look of utter dismay. "We can't. It is far too interesting to smelt."

"Interesting it might be, but we don't want to get caught with it, do we? Remember, it's not that long ago the sheriff was keen to tie you to Protestant Heresy. I don't think we should remind him of that," Matthew warned, shaking his head.

"Tell me, how did Leggy come across it?" Myles asked, inserting the key again and beginning to turn it.

"It was in a wooden case, and the whole thing was wrapped in greased hide. Leggy Dodds was at the docks helping to unload the *Santa Julia*. That was on the top of a pile of cargo when they lowered a heavy wooden coffer to the quay, a shackle block split, and the coffer smashed into the dockside. Men scattered left and right, and Leggy Dodds helped himself to that box in the confusion and disappeared. Mark my words; someone is going to miss it," Matthew stated bluntly, a solid forefinger prodding the top of the gold ornamented panel, his touch smearing the golden sheen.

"Well, for the moment, I've a mind to keep it," Myles said, pressing the lever again and watching the wheels turn.

Matthew shook his head and, rising, said, "I'll leave you alone with your child's toy."

"It's unfortunate for Leggy that he didn't see what was inside?" Myles said, smiling.

Matthew shook his head. "True. If he'd managed to work out how the catch on the box worked and seen the gold, he'd not have sold it to you for a groat."

The box the mechanism fitted into sat on the desk. The top of the box was inlaid with mother of pearl, the design a multi-pointed star pierced by an arrow. The catch on the outside was simple, but it had beaten poor Leggy. There was no lock as such. It had to be said it was not a particularly anonymous box.

Myles reluctantly put the mechanism back and closed the lid. He needed to do other things; playing with this wouldn't get them done.

Without disturbing the desk's contents, Amica jumped up, tail end flicking in the air. The cat regarded him with calm yellow eyes.

"And where have you been?" Myles asked the cat.

His answer was an arched back, and the cat leaned against his arm. Myles ignored it for a moment, then relenting, he ran a ringed hand along the cat's back; the animal purred and pressed harder against his touch. Myles smiled; the cat's faultless glossy black fur looked good beneath the line of rings on his right hand, emphasising the shine of the rubies and diamonds. The cat moved closer, intent on making its way into his lap and beginning to press against his shoulder.

"Not today, Amica. I do not need you to make me look like I've been groomed with a hackle comb," Myles scooped the mildly annoyed cat from his desk, dropped it gently on the floor, and attempted to dust stray hairs from his sleeve.

The cat looked at him for a long moment. Realising it had been dismissed, it sauntered across the room, tail erect, the tip flicking from side-to-side, before arriving at the foot of the giant bed that dominated the room. Silently and without apparent effort, it went from floor to bed and began to pluck at the pillows before settling on the duck-down, regarding him across the room with yellow eyes.

Myles pointed a long, thin finger at the cat. "As long as you do not leave any of your wastrel mice in there again, we can remain friends."

The cat meowed, its tail flicking gently on the pillow, and continued to regard him.

"Good. I am glad we are in agreement," Myles said, returning his gaze to the desk. His attention wandered back to the mother-of-pearl box, and a straying hand began to lift the lid. Could it be a music box?

Leave it!

He had other matters that needed his attention. The "child's toy" would have to wait until later – although Myles was pretty sure it was much more than that.

Myles' bookkeeper had been murdered a few months ago, and since then, it had become an annoying necessity to take on part of the dead man's role. The bookkeeper had been systematically robbing him, so now he totalled all the ledgers and prepared the bill amounts for his clerk, Peter, to produce.

A lucrative contract at the moment was providing internment for the bodies of the Parish. The sweating sickness had gripped London for the past year and provided him with a seemingly never-ending stream of unfortunates to dispose of. Thomas Clegg was Myles' man, and he kept a tally record each week of those that had been disposed of, and from that, Myles prepared the numbers for the bills.

Myles found Clegg's record on his desk and pulled it towards him.

The numbers of the deceased were about the same as the previous week, which was good, but the number of children comprised a greater number of the total than usual. Myles scowled at the tally sheet – not for any reason related to compassion for those young lost souls, but simply because the parish only paid him half the fee for a child that they paid for an adult burial. The totals for the week were twenty-six adults and eighteen children.

Myles' pen hovered over the sheet of paper.

One corner of his mouth twitched to a smile, and he applied the pen to the page and wrote –

Thirty-one adults and thirteen children

Myles put the pen down and regarded his revised numbers, tugging at his lower lip thoughtfully. Crinnion, the Parish Clerk, would argue the bill was wrong, and Myles would need to make some concession to keep him, if not happy, at least compliant. If he conceded to an error of five, then he was sure the clerk would be satisfied with his success, and Myles would still be significantly better off. Smiling and picking up the pen, he struck through the earlier line and wrote beneath it –

Thirty-six adults and eight children

The sweating sickness, sadly, would come to an end, Myles lamented. It was good for trade in some areas and not in others. More goods that he could profit from were arriving in his pawn shops that would never be reclaimed, there were more bodies to be disposed of, and the price of labour in the city had increased. Myles provided a small army of workers, the increase in costs was only partially passed on to the labourers. But the other side was that his taverns were not selling as much food and ale, and he loaned money, and the death of one of his debtors was like an arrow blow to his chest.

Painful.

He'd been lucky; he kept trying to tell himself. He had only lost two this month, and they had nearly repaid their loans. But still, it was a profit gone, and the situation was worsened by the fact that both of the deceased had belonged to a different parish, so Myles couldn't even profit from disposing of their bodies.

And then there was Garrison Bennett.

Bennett was his main rival in London; he ran similar businesses, controlled the streets in approximately half of the city, and trouble erupted where their territories met. Not at the moment, though. There was an uneasy feeling, and Myles was sure it was a temporary truce between them. Some months ago, Bennett had tried to rid the world of Myles Devereux by attempting to link him to Heresy; the scheme had failed, and Myles had proof of Bennett's involvement. So, they were both careful of each other for the moment, and hostilities had ceased. But it wouldn't last. Myles knew Bennett too well. He'd try to claim some of Myles' territory sooner or later. And given that Finch had told him he had sold beer to Bennett this time may well have arrived.

Then there was Tasker.

Once a monk, but after old Henry had ransacked the monasteries, Tasker had found himself ousted. The comfortable life he had made for himself ended.

Quickly, as a matter of personal convenience, Tasker had shrugged off his monkish robes and swapped them for those of the affluent merchant. He'd used his stolen wealth to buy several businesses scattered across the city. Some were in Bennett's territory and some in Devereux's. He paid his dues, and both men let him continue his business.

Tasker wanted to see Devereux. Myles had little liking for the man, but he paid Devereux around twenty pounds a year, and that was a significant amount of money. Tasker was due this afternoon, and Devereux was not looking forward to the meeting.

Myles pulled his wine glass towards him, dipping a finger into the wine in the cup, and he swirled the liquid. He watched the light from the candle play erratically on the disturbed surface. It was like the sun on the sea. He couldn't see the bottom of the glass. He'd always wondered why it was the some rivers where you could see the pebbles clearly through the rushing water, make out the reeds and even the fish, but when the water got deeper, you could see nothing.

Like the sea, if you stood on a cliff and looked down, as he had at Salcombe, you could see only the wave tops, the darkness of the water concealing everything below. And what, he wondered thoughtfully, was being concealed from him now? What unwanted truth was hiding below the surface, unseen?

CHAPTER THREE

Before his meeting, Myles changed his doublet for another that was equally extravagant but not as favoured as the one Finch had launched an assault on. The sleeves of the new one were paned with delicate twists of red silk bound with a silver thread, the front adorned with a double row of ruby buttons held fast in silver settings.

Tasker was shown into Myles' room. Myles ran his eyes over the man and smiled. It wasn't, however, a smile of welcome. Myles was happy with what he saw. Tasker was dressed in a mix of garments that failed to do little but make him stand out. He always appeared like a man who had stolen the clothes that hung from his body. On this occasion, they were too small.

The bulging belly, earned during his time in a monastery, had swollen further, placing a continuous strain on his doublet fastenings. Tasker's usual outer layer had been a brown, slightly stained, knee-length merchants cloak trimmed with a fox fur collar that looked as if it had provided a meal for the moths on more than one occasion. The merchants cloak was now gone. Instead, he had a waist-length one attached to one shoulder, inlaid with yellow silk that clashed violently with his green doublet. The colours should have complimented each other, but they didn't. It was like staring at the sun, and the fat monk was in the middle of the glaring drapery.

Myles also noted that although Tasker might have spent much of his money with a tailor, his cobbler had not fared so well. His boots were of a style long since abandoned in London. The overly long boot tops were turned down, the leather was grazed and cracked, and the stitching was beginning to fray. Myles could only assume they were comfortable, for why else would a man house his feet on display inside such leather monstrosities.

"It is good to see you," Myles lied, an arm gesturing towards a plush chair to the right of the fire.

Tasker took the offered seat with much aplomb. Unclipping his short cloak, he swung it over the chair back, annoyingly inside out, so the yellow lining glared at Myles, and then lowered himself into the chair, which, Myles noted, creaked at his arrival. In his bulging great doublet, he looked, backed by the sickly yellow, like a bullfrog on an ageing lily pad. Myles lowered himself into the opposite chair, lolling backwards, his long legs outstretched, crossed at the ankles. Polished Italian leather sat next to Tasker's faded, cracked grey.

Myles steepled his fingers. "How can I help?"

"Always too quick to get to the point," Tasker said, smiling and wagging a finger at him.

Myles shrugged. "Would it make such a difference if we preceded this conversation with the triviality of the weather? The health, or otherwise, of the city? The value of the coins in our purses?"

Tasker grinned. "You don't change."

Myles' gaze had travelled back to his new boots, exquisitely expensive and as glossy-black as Amica's fur. "I do change, Tasker, like a hazel bow. I am supple and happy to bend whichever way the weather takes me."

Tasker nodded his head. "I agree, adaptability is the key at the moment. We no longer live in constant times. There is much that cannot be relied upon. As Mark told us, we need to change our inner self and our old way of thinking, seek God's purpose and believe in the good news."

Myles smiled and said dryly, "I hardly think Mark was referring to a mechanism for commerce."

Tasker tapped the side of his nose with a podgy forefinger. "We all must strive to do our best. I agree running a tavern may be contrary to scripture. I was cast from the Order, and I believe the Lord has placed me to help the common man. I provide work and food for many souls. I might no longer preach in a church, Devereux, but I can exert the Lord's influence over more now than before. I have changed my inner way of thinking and accepted that this was a course planned for me by the Lord."

"A veritable disciple," Myles said, his tone blatantly sarcastic.

"You scoff!" Tasker laughed. "But I believe I have been placed here for the good of man. You'll see, I am guided by the Lord and protected by him." Tasker continued, then changing his tone, his voice grave, he pronounced, "which brings me to the reason for my visit."

Myles smiled. "Come on then, we've talked trivialities as you wished. Get to the point."

"It's a matter of money if you must know," Tasker said.

"It usually is," Myles said, his eyes still on his feet, his tone bored. Inside, though, a warm, pleased feeling was welling from his stomach – Tasker was about to ask him for a loan, which would be both sizeable and profitable.

Tasker leaned forward, attempting to reclaim Myles' wandering attention. "I'm paying you and Bennett, as you know, to ensure my own business runs smoothly, and it does. I have no problems with either of you and I am making a healthy profit."

"I'm glad to hear it," Myles said, his tone offhand.

"So much so that I am looking for something else to do. I want to build on what I have, and the Lord has provided me with the means to do this." Tasker held a clenched fist up. "Into my hands, he has delivered the means, and I must act on his will."

Not a loan, then? Myles hid his disappointment and asked, "And what is the Lord's will?"

"Into these poor hands, the Lord has placed his trust, and I will not disappoint him. I shall strive to carry out his wishes." Tasker held his fat, pale hands, palm up and empty, Myles noted, apart from a long line of rings that wrapped every finger.

"And the Lord's wishes are?" Myles enquired, folding his hands in his lap.

Tasker sat back in the chair, and Myles winced as the wooden joints gave an audible complaint. "It is simply this: I wish to expand my business, employ more men, provide more work for the poor."

Myles raised an eyebrow. "And they, in turn, can provide you with a profit?"

Tasker wagged a finger at Myles again and, smiling, said, "you are ever the cynic. My work is God's, but I'll allow you your jest."

"I'm not a cynic, Tasker. I just see the world as it truly is," Myles replied dryly.

"To think anything but God controls the world goes against the scriptures," Tasker said, a note of reprimand in his voice. "You need to open your heart to God, humble yourself to his power and then you will feel the joy of his touch."

"It's not Sunday, Tasker, and I have no wish to be preached to," Myles said, his voice cold.

Tasker smiled. "It is the will of the Lord for me to show you the way to his fold. I cannot discard a lifetime of faith."

Tasker bestowed a benevolent smile on Myles, and it took all his self-control to not return it with a scowl. The hands in his lap were white knuckled with the effort. "Why did you wish to see me?"

"I've heard a rumour that you are looking at moving overseas, leaving London," Tasker said simply.

Myles' body stiffened. The muscles in his legs tightened, and the boots twitched, but he made no move apart from that. His face was impassive. An acute observer might have seen the light tremble in the facets of the ruby on his right hand, but they would have had to have stood close to him and not blinked. Tasker missed all of this and continued to smile at Myles.

"It is understandable as well; the past few months have not been kind to you, and after that, a man could persuade himself that remaining in the city was not a good course of action." Tasker was referring to an incident three months past when the queen's men were searching for Myles to arrest him for Heresy and Treason. It had been a narrow escape.

"And if you recall, I was exonerated," Myles replied tersely.

"True, and quite rightly so. But it would be natural if you wished to leave London. I am sure it would have been a trial on your nerves," Tasker said.

Myles, who did not like being discussed at all, said coldly, "every man has a price, Tasker, even I."

Tasker smiled broadly. "I'd heard right then. Rumour has it you have contacts in France, family even, and London bores you, which I can understand."

Myles forced a smile onto his lips and took a long, slow breath, forcing himself to still his temper.

"London would bore any man after a while," Myles replied quietly. The fingers of his left hand had found the ruby ring on his right and were twisting it slowly.

"So, a price, do you have one in mind?" Tasker asked.

Myles let his eyes rest on Tasker's face for a moment. "For everything?

Tasker licked his lips. "Everything."

Myles smiled. "Make me an offer."

Tasker's brow furrowed. It was obviously not the answer he had wanted. "I don't know the full extent of what you have, so I am not in a position to blindly make an offer, sir. I would risk jeopardizing myself or insulting you."

"And you wouldn't want to do that, would you?" Myles said, rising suddenly. He had suffered enough of this conversation and didn't want it to continue.

Tasker was left to scramble back to his feet. "I had no wish to annoy you, sir. I can see my words have done that."

"Not at all, Tasker, as I said, make me an offer," Myles replied, stepping towards the door and tapping lightly on the oak. A second later, it opened, and Matthew appeared. The conversation was over.

Tasker, his worn boots taking him towards the door, was forced to take his leave of Myles. "I shall be in touch .... soon."

Myles let the door close, listening to the sound of Matthew escorting Tasker across the outer room and heading down the stairs into the tap room of the White Hart. When he was sure he was gone, Myles yanked open the door.

"Matthew, get in here. *Now!*" Myles let the door go and stalked across the room, his hands behind his back, watching Tasker leave the yard of the White Hart from the open window.

"What did Tasker want?" Matthew said, closing the door behind him.

Myles waited to reply. He was still watching Tasker, mounted and followed by his retinue, leave the yard. As he rode through the gates, he turned and looking up, caught Myles' eyes and waved.

Myles raised a hand in reply, but there was no smile on his lips. Turning towards Matthew. "That shit has heard I am selling my business and leaving London! How did he hear that?"

"Tasker hasn't the coin or the intelligence," Matthew said, then added, "are you sure he was serious?"

Myles turned and regarded Matthew with a furious gaze. "He was completely serious. Which has to mean one of a few things."

"Go on ...." Matthew said, tucking his thumbs into the top of his broad belt.

"There is a rumour that I'm looking to leave London, or the arrogant bastard has the effrontery to think I could be tempted by his coin or ...." Myles paused and turned to Matthew. "Someone else has a hold of his strings."

Matthew, ever calm, had a thoughtful expression on his face. "Well, it's not that long ago that, for a moment, it did look as if you would leave London. There was a warrant for your arrest if you recall?"

"Why do people feel the need to keep reminding me? I have hardly forgotten! It was months ago, and we've made sure since it is well known that we are in control, haven't we?" Myles said, rounding on Matthew.

"We have, but that rumour will still be there. You might not be wanted by the queen's men anymore, but no one will forget that you nearly fell from grace, will they?" Matthew pointed out unnecessarily.

Myles glared at him. It wasn't the response he'd wanted. "Alright, I accept, in Tasker's mind, that he may feel I am still willing to leave the city. But why leave it for three months? Why was he not on my doorstep when they raised the cry of Heretic? Surely that would have been the time to act?"

Matthew shrugged. "It would have been, but who knows what's on Tasker's mind? He might have been waiting to see if you would still fall. If you did, he'd have no need to part with his gold, would he?"

"Maybe," Myles admitted grudgingly, then added, "see what you can find out."

"I will. Do you have the numbers for Peter? If he writes up the bills, I'll deliver them to the Parish today as well," Matthew asked, his eyes scanning the desk.

"Here." Myles fished the paper off the desk and held it towards Matthew.

Looking at the sheet with the amended line, Matthew shook his head. "Crinnion is not going to be happy."

"I don't care what his state of mind is, you are right, he'll be unhappy, we will concede to a generous adjustment of five, he will enjoy his fleeting moment of victory, and we will be paid. It'll serve the shit right for trying to trade with Carson," Myles said contemptuously. He'd caught the clerk sending bodies to another to dispose of a few months ago, and since then, he'd been keeping the clerk on a tight leash.

"I'm sure you are right," Matthew said, leaving Myles alone.

Myles' blood was still boiling.

Tasker's business was the same as Devereux's. How dare he assert that he ran his for the good of the common man?

Tasker was motivated by greed, the same as all men. Holding his business up as having some divine connection was an affront. The shit held his business up as if it were some holy institution. You'd think to listen to him that he was going on a bloody crusade with God at his right hand.

CHAPTER FOUR

A messenger from the Parish Clerk, Crinnion, requesting his urgent attention regarding the settlement of a bill, arrived. Myles smiled, and the messenger was sent back to his master with the unsatisfactory reply that Myles Devereux would attend his master in his own good time. It was a matter of money, so Myles would go the following day and resolve the issue of his miscounting of the parish's dead. But until then, Crinnion could wait.

The inlaid box caught his eye. It was beautiful. Myles' long fingers brushed the top; the mother-of-pearl decoration was wonderfully smooth and cool. His hand hesitated for a moment, then with a grin, he pressed the diamond on the side and released the lid. His smile broadened. What was it?

He lifted it out from the box and placed it on the desk; seating himself, he gazed at it. Intricate, made with skill, and for an unknown purpose. He couldn't ask Mya; that would be to reveal that he had it, and that wasn't safe. Mya, the Jewish usurer, might be an expert in all things made of gold, but he wasn't to be trusted. Whatever it was, it had a significant value, and whoever it belonged to would be missing it. He had no doubt of that.

One name had been wandering around his mind for a while.

Chance is a Game

    Fitzwarren. An irreverent and highly dangerous mercenary. He'd known him for years, and recently, he had provided a service for him. Fitzwarren's brother had found his way into the Tower dungeon, and Myles had provided the black powder and entry to the fortress so he could retrieve him. But was Fitzwarren still in the city? If he had any sense, he wouldn't be. Myles hadn't been present when he had retrieved his brother from the Tower, but he'd certainly heard about the explosion. All the windows in the Beachamp Tower had been blown out, and a large quantity of new wood for flooring was set on fire. But you never knew with Fitzwarren, where he was or what he was thinking. Evasion was to him second nature.

    Making a sudden decision, Myles closed the box and sent a summons to the last place he knew Fitzwarren had been seen. Myles was delighted and, at the same time, surprised when it was answered only a few hours later.

    The mercenary was richly dressed, the colour dark, chosen no doubt to ensure he did not stand out at first glance, but his clothes still marked him as nobility. Myles knew his father had disowned him, but he was still Richard Fitzwarren, son of Lord Fitzwarren, the old king's councillor and confidante. Any second glance would easily confirm that. The fur trim on his cloak was from a marten or sable, the boots were side laced, and the leather cut through with fine silver thread. The doublet was artful, and Myles' eyes made note of the design. The slashes that would typically leak the shirt's brighter colour below showed a blue velvet, as dark and rich as a bruised summer sky during a storm. Sewn into the velvet, starlike, were cold diamonds in silver settings. The effect was subtle, but once you'd seen them, it was impossible to ignore them, capturing the light from the room and sending it back tenfold from the jeweller's finely cut facets. Could Drew, his tailor, produce something as rich as this, Myles wondered?

"I am amazed you are still in London," Myles said, meeting Fitzwarren's cold grey gaze.

"Is that the only reason you requested my presence? Just to find out?" Fitzwarren, uninvited, settled down in one of the chairs near the fire. His feet crossed at the ankles, and an inquisitive Amica, Myles was annoyed to see, began paying court to his boots.

"A cat!" Fitzwarren, sounding delighted, lifted Amica into his lap.

"It's London, we have rats," Myles said dryly.

One corner of Fitzwarren's mouth curled into a wry smile, his eyes on the animal, he said, "I would lay a wager that this mouser has a name."

"I didn't ask you here to discuss vermin control," Myles, stepping forward, scooped the animal from Fitzwarren's lap and deposited it roughly onto the floor, where Amica regarded him with an annoyed stare and a mewl of disapproval.

"I thought so," Fitzwarren said, then added. "Don't take your annoyance at me out on your cat, Devereux."

"You'd bring out the worst in a saint," Myles growled.

"It has been said," Fitzwarren replied. The cat, in an act of rebellion, had returned to his lap and was regarding Myles with a cold stare. "Why did you want me? I was about to leave London another day, and you would have missed me."

"Is that so," Myles said, still annoyed.

"Yes, so get to the point, Devereux," Fitzwarren said, smoothing the cat's fur with a ringed hand.

Myles rose and stalked to the desk, picking up the box. "It's this. I want to know what it is?"

Fitzwarren, a furrow between his brows, gently deposited the cat on the floor and rose, joining Myles. "Well, it's a box. Does it open?"

Myles, ignoring Fitzwarren's sarcastic tone, pressed the diamond. Set the box on the desk and lifted out the gold mechanism.

Fitzwarren just stared silently at it.

"What?" Myles said, his gaze switching between the glittering golden trinket and Fitzwarren's face.

"Does it work?" Was all Fitzwarren said, an outstretched hand turning it so he could view it better.

"I'd have to know what it is before answering that question. There is a key here." Myles fished the golden key out of the bottom of the box and handed it to Fitzwarren. "It fits in the side."

Fitzwarren's attention was wholly on the box. He inserted the key and turned it slowly, listening to the mechanism as the cogs and springs inside moved.

"What are you listening for?" Myles said impatiently.

"Shush ...." Fitzwarren continued to turn the key. "There we are. Did you hear it?"

"Hear what?" Myles said.

"When it is fully wound, you can hear a final louder click when one of the wheels inside has reached its final position. You need to be careful. If you pressure it beyond this point, you can ...."

"Yes .... but what is it?" Myles interrupted.

"Will you have a little patience? Let me see .... Ah, here we are. When were you born?" Fitzwarren announced, looking up.

"What!" Myles blurted.

"Not a difficult question, when?" Fitzwarren asked again.

"What's that got to do with anything?" Myles said hotly.

"Alright, let's suppose you were born under the sign of ...." Fitzwarren paused, smiled, and said. "You are a little vain, so let's assume Venus is your ruling planet, which makes you a Virgo."

Myles scowled and watched as Fitzwarren rotated the outer wheel by hand, saying, "So that puts you between August 22nd and September 23rd, or is it the 24th? I can't remember rightly. So, to be safe, let's select September 1st."

As Myles watched, Fitzwarren set the outer wheel; lifting his hands from the box, he asked. "Are you ready?"

"Ready for what?" Myles said, sounding confused.

"To have your horoscope cast." Fitzwarren pressed the small lever on the outside, and the inner wheels began to turn, the box emitting delicate sounds from the moving mechanism. The wheels slowed, then, with a final click, stopped.

Myles looked from the box to Fitzwarren. "That's it? So what do these inner wheels tell you?"

Fitzwarren bent his head over the box, brow furrowed, and then announced. "I see a short life, brought to an end by incaution and arrogance .... how should I know? Do I look like a caster of horoscopes?"

"You know how it works," Myles said accusingly.

"I know how it works because I've seen one before. Granted, the one I saw was not as grand as this. I believe these are called Astrologica or astrologiae arca if you prefer the Latin," Fitzwarren said, then added, "and this one must be worth a small fortune. Where did you get it from?"

"I bought it for a groat," Myles said and was satisfied to see Fitzwarren's face contort with genuine shock.

"A groat!" Fitzwarren blurted.

"Why? Do you think I paid too much?" Myles replied, a wicked smile on his face.

"I would imagine whoever it belongs to is missing it very much. I would be careful who you show this to, Devereux," Fitzwarren advised.

"You are, apart from Matthew, the only person who has seen it," Myles replied.

"Apart from the man who sold it to you for a groat." Fitzwarren corrected.

Myles shook his head. "The fool couldn't get the box to open."

"Well, I would keep this treasure close, and if you want to sell it be very careful. Remember, Devereux, it's not very long ago that you were tainted with Heresy, and this," Fitzwarren said, his finger tapping one of the gold wheels, "can be viewed as Heresy. Man should not predict the future; that is for God alone to preside over."

"Why does every man I meet need to remind me of recent past events," Myles said, annoyed.

"Probably because you can be, on occasion, incautious," Fitzwarren replied.

"I have a mind to keep it," Myles said, ignoring Fitzwarren's comment and turning the box towards him.

Fitzwarren said, chuckling, "It could serve you well should you ever lose your business."

"Where have you seen one of these before?" Myles asked.

"Cambridge, when I was briefly at University. John Dee, have you heard of him?" Fitzwarren asked.

"You know Dee?" Myles said.

"Not very well. It's a long story, but I was forced to take an examination in mathematics, and Dee provided tutoring in this subject. Without him, I doubt I would have passed," Fitzwarren said.

"I thought you were studying philosophy and never finished because your father stopped paying," Myles said accusingly. "Make your mind up."

"I was. I took the examination in mathematics for another student called Neephouse. I didn't do it for kindness either, I did it for money," Fitzwarren replied, an edge of irritation had crept into his usually calm voice.

"So, in fact, you did obtain a qualification, even if you can't lay claim to it," Myles chuckled, shaking his head. "And Dee, he showed you how to use this?"

"Not really. Dee had one, and it is based on a mathematical concept that Dee believes underpins the whole universe, and he used it to explain that concept to me. So I can show you how it works, but I couldn't tell you what it purports to say," Fitzwarren replied.

"Could it belong to Dee?" Myles asked.

"It could, and it also might be that he'd recognise it, but asking him comes with the danger of revealing your possession of it," Fitzwarren said, then fishing in his purse, found five gold Angels and laid them on the desk. "Payment for the powder, thank you again."

"You are leaving London? Where to next?" Myles asked.

Fitzwarren smiled. "You don't honestly expect me to answer that, do you?"

Myles shrugged. "I thought you might have tried to ingratiate yourself with your father again while you were here?"

"Why?" Fitzwarren asked bluntly.

"He's rich. Would it not be easier to court him than earn an uncertain income on another shore? I know which choice I would be making," Myles replied.

"My father might be Lord Fitzwarren, but I doubt that there's any gain to be made there," Fitzwarren replied dryly.

"Why, have you tried?" Myles said.

"Myles, give up. I'm not going to be reconciled with my father, now or at any time in the future," Richard Fitzwarren said, a mild note of irritation creeping into his voice.

"You recently advised me that I was prone to vanity. Are you not falling prey to this sin as well?" Myles said.

"It is not vanity. The bastard tried to kill me. That wasn't something he did by accident, folly, or mistake. His decision was not guided by miscalculation; it was made on the simple premise that his life, and the life of his preferred son, Robert, would be vastly improved without me. So not vanity, Devereux," Richard Fitzwarren said. "And stop trying to rouse my bloody temper simply because your cat prefers my lap to yours."

Myles' expression froze. Fitzwarren's words were a little too accurate.

"Exactly, vanity, as I recently said, is your flaw, not mine," Fitzwarren said, his voice calm again, and with a slight smile on his face he lifted the pleased cat from the floor, his eyes on the animal he asked. "And her name is?"

"Amic ...." Myles stopped himself as soon as he realised the trap he had just fallen into.

"Ah, Amica. So now you have at least one friend," Fitzwarren handed him the cat. "Treat your friends well, Devereux. You never know when you may need them."

Myles watched him leave shortly after, then through the open window, watched his horse leave the White Hart. Sighing, Myles stowed the Astrologica, as he now knew it was, back inside its box.

CHAPTER FIVE

"What did you find out about Tasker?" Myles asked.

Matthew pulled the bonnet from his head and placed it on the table. "Well, Tasker seems not just interested in your business. In the last few months, he's bought the Black Swan on Newbold Street and further out, near West Field Marsh, the Saints Inn."

Myles, suddenly interested, sat up straight in his chair. "Has he indeed. That must have cost him a bit. Where's he got his sudden wealth from?"

Matthew shook his head. "That question I can't answer. Both of those two taverns give him a wedge between you and Bennett in the West of the city. It's not controlling as much of the area as you and Bennett are, but if you think about it, that greatly increases his influence. I know he's paying dues to both you and Bennett to continue with his business, but the question is, how long does he want to keep doing this?"

Myles sat back in the chair. It was true. If you held a tavern on a street, that was akin to being the king on a throne in terms of the surrounding area. They were pivotal for trade, crucial meeting places for men and merchants and many flanked markets or hosted their own. The more taverns you controlled, the more wealth generally you could command. "How many Inns does that give him now?"

"Too many," came Matthew's blunt reply; leaning forward, he reclaimed his bonnet from the table and fitted it back to his head. "I think Tasker needs his wings clipping."

"First, though, I'd like to find out what he's up to. Why did he want to buy my business? I said I'd meet with him in a few days, and perhaps I will," Myles replied thoughtfully, his arms folded across his chest and forefinger tapping the sleeve of his doublet.

"Why?" Matthew asked, his bushy brows merging with his frown.

"He wants me to give him a price," Myles said.

"You are not going to give him one, are you?" Matthew said, his voice flooded with sudden concern.

Myles smiled evilly. "Why not. Remember, everyone and everything has a price, even me. Let's see just how much gold Tasker really has."

Matthew tilted his head to one side. "Fair enough. Just watch him; I don't trust him." Then, changing the subject, he said, "are you going to see Crinnion today? You've put it off longer than you should have."

Myles scowled, waving his hand. "Yes, yes."

Shortly afterwards, Myles, his usual escort behind him, and Matthew at his side rode through the London streets to the parish offices.

Crinnion was less than pleased to see Devereux's men arrive, and Myles knew it.

Myles stalked into Crinnion's office, heeled the door closed behind him and slapped his riding gloves down hard, sending an ordered pile of paper to scatter across the desk.

Crinnion yelped and tried to save his work.

Myles rolled his eyes. "When you are quite finished, do you want to tell me why you have summoned me to your offices? I would like to remind you, Crinnion, that the parish owes me money and not vice versa."

"It's regarding the payment, sir. I feel there is an error …." Crinnion stammered, placing his retrieved papers at the other end of the desk and, for security, putting a heavy inkpot on top of them.

"An error on your part?" Myles said, walking around the desk and dropping into the clerk's chair.

"No, not …. our error. There seems to be some …. confusion on your bill, sir," Crinnion stammered, clearly not enjoying the conversation.

"Confusion," Myles pronounced the word like a threat.

"Err …. yes …. you see we, I mean I, think there were more children than you have stated on your bill, and obviously, the parish pays more for adult internments," Crinnion managed.

Myles regarded him with a cold stare. "Are you sure? Show me?"

Crinnion dug briskly through his pile of papers. "I had it to hand, but it has been mixed up with others …." He continued to leaf through the pages. "Here it is."

Crinnion passed the bill to Devereux. Devereux read the numbers out loud.

Thirty-six adults and eight children

"There should have been more children and less adults," Crinnion said.

Myles dropped the sheet on the desk. "It is difficult to determine adult from child. Some are sewn in shrouds, so how can you tell? My men may have made an error. What do your records state the numbers should have been?"

"Umm, well, we don't have a weekly total, as such, just the church records, and, of course, it might be that the dates recorded in their ledgers are after the bodies have been collected, so it is very hard to determine which would belong to which week," Crinnion admitted, a weak smile on his face.

Myles forced himself not to grin. Crinnion had just told him exactly what he wanted to know. "So, how do you know that this bill is wrong?"

"I just …. there …. more …. usually, it would be more children. Eight is very low," Crinnion stammered.

"Fewer children in the parish have lost their poor infant souls, and you are bewailing the fact?" Myles said, his voice suddenly shocked. "I would have thought this would be a cause for celebration, that the children were spared."

"That's not what I meant," Crinnion tried, his face contorted with the strain of the conversation.

"It is what it sounds like, My God! You'd rather bury infants," Myles said, now sounding thoroughly shocked, regarding Crinnion with wide eyes.

"Sir, that is not what I meant, simply that there had been a miscount," Crinnion stammered, mottled colour suffused the clerk's face.

Myles was quite aware that very soon, Crinnion would take the offer Myles would place before him to end this confrontation. His hands flat on the clerk's desk, he leaned towards him. "Surely you know *exactly* how many of the parish's dead you hand into my care?"

"As I said …. the records from the church are not made out immediately, so there …. sometimes …. well, it is often the case that the unfortunate parishioners are collected before the records are completed," Crinnion said weakly.

Myles straightened and folded his arms, a look of complete dismay on his face. "So you are telling me that, as Parish Clerk, you've failed to keep adequate records for your masters? And you've dared to claim an error on my part when you have no idea at all whether my bill is correct or not?"

Crinnion opened his mouth, thought better of it, and snapped it shut.

"I don't think the parish councillors will be too pleased to find this out, do you? I keep records, Crinnion, and this bill," Myles stabbed the page on the desk, "agrees with them. This bill stands unless you can prove that it should be otherwise."

Crinnion's eyes followed Myles' hand down to the page.

Myles waited for a moment before delivering the salvation Crinnion was praying for. "So, shall I leave this matter in your hands, and if you produce evidence to the contrary, I will review it?"

Crinnion swallowed hard. "Yes, yes, that would be acceptable."

"Good," Myles said, turning and hiding a smile. If the idiot clerk couldn't keep adequate records, he deserved to be taken advantage of, and now he had confessed that there was very little chance that the documents could be validated. Myles had no intention of revising his figures. Crinnion would fear losing his position, especially if it became known he had lost parish funds due to his poor record-keeping. Myles also knew he could continue to twist the weekly numbers on the bills to his advantage and make a little more profit for longer without Crinnion's interference. It was turning out to be another good day, despite the poor weather.

Susie curtsied clumsily as she passed, her eyes fixed on the floor and her arms around the basket she was carrying. Myles stopped, smiled, and took two quick steps back. Not many months ago, she had saved him from being crushed beneath a falling crowd.

"I've still a rib or two that hurt on occasion," Myles said, a hand on the right side of his chest.

"Better to hurt, sir, than not to. It's God's way of telling you that you are alive," she replied, her eyes avoiding his.

Myles laughed. "That's a truth. What are you carrying?"

"I'm taking bread to the tavern, sir," Susie replied.

Myles reached inside the basket, resting the back of his hand against one of the small loaves he found it still warm and took it from the basket. Closing his eyes momentarily, he inhaled the scent of the bread. "Best smell in London."

"It's the best smell, but not if you've had an empty stomach for a week 'an no hope of filling it. Then it's the smell o' Hell," Susie replied.

Myles caught her eye for a moment. "You're not still hungry, are you?"

"I've a full belly, a skeen over me' poor head to keep me dry and silva in ma pocket.

Myles raised an eyebrow. "Honest coin?"

Susie hitched the basket onto her hip, loosened an arm, and thumped him good-naturedly. "It was yours once, but I earned it honestly."

Myles smiled and helped himself to another piece of bread. "I am sure you did."

Myles left her and set off up the stairs; he was halfway up when, with the speed of an arrow, Amica, pursued by the tavern's fat tabby, flew screeching across the inn. Speed was not on her side, and the tabby launched, landing on her back. The two cats rolled across the floor in a shrieking black, brown and white ball, locked together by tooth and claw. The fight was a matter of a moment; the victor, the tabby, jumped to a tabletop, arched backed, and hissing and Amica, still screeching, fled through the open tavern door. Myles bestowed the tavern mouser with an evil glare.

Myles found out very quickly where the cat had fled when he opened the door to his room. Amica, trembling, was sitting on his windowsill. Myles picked her up, examined the sliced ear, and, looking at the cat squarely in the face, said, "there's a lesson for you. Don't stray into another's territory. That filthy mog would have its arse kicked if it came up here, and it knows it, so you, keep out of its way."

The cat mewled. Myles stroked a hand down the cat's back and deposited it on the rug near the fire.

He couldn't recall when the cat appeared on his lap during the evening. Tired, he'd fallen asleep, a hand on the furry black animal. The fire burnt down, and Myles, wearing only a linen shirt, was woken by the cold fingers of the night. Amica was curled asleep on his chest. Lifting the cat from him, he rose and went to the bed. Myles deposited the cat on a pillow on the opposite side.

The cat's eyes opened, watching him as he slewed off his shirt and pulled the hose from his legs, dropping them on the floor next to the bed. Folding the covers back, he slid between them. He'd been in his room all evening, and none of the servants would enter when he was present. Myles preferred to entertain the notion that only he and those few he invited in ever stepped through the doorway. So, the bed hadn't been warmed; it was a cold price to pay for his solitude.

The fire had burnt down and was doing little to defeat the cold air of the night rolling through the open shutters. But Myles liked them open; he wanted to see the dim light of night through them, the stars, the moon, the dark vista of London. But he also liked the comfort of the escape. Below, the yard was guarded; Myles didn't fear an assailant viewing his open window as an invitation. Like Amica, he could, and had in the past, made a quick exit through the window, onto the ledge of the jutting roof below and then it was a short drop into the yard. He knew from bitter experience that it was never wise to be in a trap with only one way out.

Myles wasn't looking forward to the meeting. He knew he would have to contain his temper if he wanted to find out what Tasker was truly up to. So, instead, he sidetracked his mind, wondering what vile concoction of fabrics the ex-monk would have swathed himself with for his next visit.

Myles was not to be disappointed.

The green doublet was gone and had been replaced by a yellow, red and somewhat worn one. Myles doubted it had been made for Tasker; it looked like a piece of court attire that had come his way. His tailor had badly altered it; the cloth hung slack in places and tight in others around his well-fed body. The slashes in the sleeves were overly long and revealed a bright yellow beneath; the cuffs were banded with a delicate lace that wear had begun to fray, straying threads attesting to use. The buttons down the front were also very wrong. Each was plain and black and stuck out from the rich, bright fabric like a row of paupers. The doublet had been made for show, probably for a specific occasion, and the original buttons, probably of significant worth, had been swapped. But Tasker obviously favoured the garment, and he strutted into Devereux's presence like an earl.

Myles was impeccably dressed in some of his tailor's finest work. Wearing a rich dark green velvet, pricked with silver studs along the sleeves and fastened down the front with a double row of emerald buttons. The green glow from the gems in perfect harmony with an expensive silk visible beneath the slashed sleeves.

If the battle were one to catch the eye, then Devereux had lost. The fact that an outcast fat monk dared to consider himself above Myles was almost too much. Feeling his temper rising, he let his eyes wander back to Tasker's impoverished buttons, and the corner of his mouth twitched into a smile.

"Tasker, it is good to see you again," Myles lied; he didn't invite the other man to take a seat but dropped into one of the comfortable fireside chairs and looked up at his guest.

For a moment, Tasker stared down at Myles, his self-assurance in sudden disarray. He lowered himself clumsily into the chair opposite Myles, his short cloak caught beneath his legs, tugging on his shoulder, and he was forced to a half-rise to pull it free from beneath him. Myles waited silently for Tasker to rearrange himself, a look of strained patience on his face.

"Did you think any more about my proposal?" Tasker asked, free of the constraints of his clothing, he leaned back in the chair.

"I did, yes. It opened up several interesting possibilities," Myles said, clasping his hands around one knee and drawing it closer.

"Indeed," Tasker licked his lips, sounding pleased.

Myles waved a hand in the air. "London is not the city it once was; the sweating sickness ever lingers, and an opportunity to be free of the threat would be welcome."

For a moment, Tasker seemed shocked.

"But as to a price, that was a more difficult decision, and I feel that I'd not like insult you, sir, by stating a figure that would be .... beyond your reach," Myles said quietly.

Chance is a Game

"I can appreciate your sentiment. However, I do have significant means, and I wish to increase my business in London. I place my faith in the Lord God to protect me from the Devil's evil that lurks in the city," Tasker said, with more than a hint of the pulpit preacher in his words.

"That must be very comforting," Myles said acidly, then added, "so, make me an offer. You will have an amount in mind, and I shall not spurn you if the figure is not to my liking."

Tasker shifted in his seat. "It is difficult to quantify. There are so many aspects to your business. Many of them would be unknown to me."

"True, and if your figure falls short of my expectations, I can enlighten you as to why the value should be greater," Myles said. "So, tell me, Master Tasker, what is my worth."

Tasker was silent for a few minutes, his breathing heavy, and the flat black buttons around his middle fought against their fixings. "I think …."

"Yes …." Myles said, leaning back in his chair, moulding himself into the plush fabric.

"I think …." Tasker licked his lips, swallowed hard, seemed to recover his composure and said overly loudly, "One hundred pounds.

There was a moment of silence.

"One hundred pounds," Myles repeated; if Tasker had looked closely enough, he would have noticed that Devereux's relaxed poise had gone, reclined he still maybe, but his muscles were tensed like a cats, and he was ready to spring from the chair.

"Yes, one hundred pounds is a generous amount," Tasker repeated, the pitch of his voice slightly increased.

"It is a notable amount, I agree if you were looking to buy horses or cattle," Myles said, forcing himself to remain in the chair, his eyes fixed on Tasker. "However, it is a little short of the required amount."

"How short?" Tasker asked; one of his hands was white-knuckled and had tightened on the chair arm.

"Well. Take your amount of one hundred pounds and increase it tenfold, and then we will have a deal," Myles said languidly"

"Ten times!" Tasker barely managed to keep his voice under control.

"Yes, ten times would secure my retreat from London, and this," Myles waved his arm around his room, "Would be yours."

"That's a thousand pounds," Tasker stated.

"Well done, your mathematics is impeccable." A hint of sarcasm had crept into Myles' voice.

Tasker was silent momentarily, and then it was Myles' turn to experience an acute shock when he spoke.

"Very well, it is a high sum, but if you can prove the worth to me of this figure, then we may have a deal," Tasker spoke slowly, nodding as he did.

Myles stared at him for a moment. "And I'll not accept it in the queen's coin."

Tasker waved a hand in the air. "And I would not expect you to, old Henry thieved half the worth from the coins. It would be a payment in gold."

"In gold," Myles repeated, fixing Tasker with a hard stare.

"Indeed, in gold," Tasker replied. For a moment, the control of the conversation had swapped.

Amica chose that moment to drop silently between the open shutters, landing on Myles' desk. Sitting, she lifted one paw, licked it, and observed both men with unwavering eyes.

"A cat?" Tasker's voice sounded shocked.

Myles returned Amica's unblinking stare and hoped the animal could read his mind. It couldn't, or if it could, it didn't want to comply with the request to leave – quickly.

"I thought the bloody kitchen mouser knew better than to come in here," Myles said, glaring at the cat. "Out, go on …."

"Are you sure? It looks very at home," Tasker said, his eyes watching the cat.

"I am not unique, in London, in having an issue with mice?" Myles said flatly and watched Amica drop from the desk, cross the room, and press against Tasker's boots.

"Can't stand the damned animals," Tasker said, removing his feet from the cat. "They are the Devil's work."

"Are they?" Myles said distractedly, not at all interested in Tasker's opinion on the feline species.

"The damnable creatures will jump from midden to mire then table …. Ahhhh," Tasker yelped and began to force his bulk up the chair back as Amica, bored with his boots, sprung up into his lap.

Tasker, raising his hand, was about to strike the cat, but Myles, quicker than the monk, rose, slipped an arm under Amica's body and lifted her from Tasker's lap before the blow could connect.

Tasker dropped back into the chair, watching Myles put the cat down near the fire. "Filthy things."

Myles, his back momentarily to Tasker, cursed silently, forced a smile back to his face and returned to his chair.

"Where were we," Myles said as he lowered himself smoothly back into the chair's embrace. "I remember. You understand I need proof of your ability to pay."

"Of course," Tasker said, brushing cat hairs from his lap, and then added, "And I would need an assurance of the worth of what I am paying for."

It was not at all as Myles had expected the conversation to go. By now, he had expected Tasker to be scuttling from his room in a flurry of soiled yellow and orange velvet with his tail firmly between his legs. But not so.

"Very well, then, enlighten me," Myles said, fixing what he hoped was a winning smile on his face to conceal his loathing for Tasker.

"My pleasure. It is a matter of some security on my part. I can arrange for you to view what I have on offer at a convenient place in a few days if that would suit you?" Tasker said, knowing he had shocked Devereux; he seemed to be enjoying the conversation now.

"Send a message when you are ready, and I will attend," Myles said, managing, with effort, to retain a disinterested tone.

Myles' eyes rested on the closed-door Tasker had just exited through. How could Tasker have access to such wealth? Was it a ruse? Was he trying to make a fool of Devereux?

Amica made her way into his lap.

"We are going to need to stalk Master Tasker very carefully," Myles said, smoothing her fur gently.

CHAPTER SIX

Matthew's shouted words didn't wake him immediately. It took another bellow and a shake of his shoulder to drag him from sleep.

"For God's sake. Get up!"

"What's happened?" Myles' eyes, sleep blurred, tried to focus on the man above him.

"The Unicorn is on fire," Matthew bellowed.

"How long?" Myles was bolt upright in a moment. Fire was one of the most feared things in the city. It fed vociferously on dried thatch and wooden timbers. Then, when its appetite was not satisfied, it would leap the small gaps between the buildings and bring down its next victim.

Fire was relentless.

"Too long, the roof is already down, and it's taken hold of the stables at the back," Matthew said, "I've already sent men across. There'll be little they can do about the fire, but they'll prevent any looting by chance scavengers."

Myles dressed quickly, pulling the cold hose he had discarded only hours before over his legs. He was sure he could smell smoke on the air that drifted through the open shutters. By the time he arrived in the yard at the back of the White Hart, his men held lit torches aloft, his horse was saddled and ready, and he knew he had not imagined the scent. London always smelt of wood smoke, cooking fires, braziers, and ovens issued a constant grey plume into the sky, but this was more. The aroma told of a smoke that was blanketing London, unseen in the dark, spreading like leaking blood, pouring along the lanes, streets, and alleys as it took the life of the Unicorn.

Myles knew that if it had been light, he'd be able to see the smoke rising into the air and drifting through London. As it was, he could just feel the assault on his eyes. The smoke was a quiet ghost and all that was left of his tavern.

Very soon, the orange glow that marked where the Unicorn had once served London could be seen. When Matthew said the roof had come in, Myles had been hopeful; sometimes, when this happened, the flames could be extinguished before they took hold of the rest of the building. It brought the fire down to where it could be trampled out. The Unicorn had not been fortunate; the fire was eating deep into the wooden timber of her walls, and the roof beams, still in place like giant blackened whale ribs against a lightening dawn sky, were feeding the flames.

"Damn!" Myles' hand tightened on the mare's reins, holding her still. The horse was stamping and agitated in the road with the smell of fire in her nostrils.

"It's too late. It's going to take the whole row out." Matthew, pulling his mount closer to Myles, pointed to the buildings next to the Unicorn. They were thatched, and the dry roofs were already ablaze. There were at least ten buildings jammed in a single row before a break where a road cut between them, and Matthew was right. There was nothing that would stop it now.

Chance is a Game

All around Myles, the street was alive with the sound of panic. Shouts of help. Screams of women, the wail of children. Belongings salvaged before the flames could claim them were heaped in the middle of the road, a spinning wheel, chairs, an upturned table, a box of wool, a baby's crib. To his right two men were hauling a coffer through the doorway of a shop, a little further down the row from the Unicorn. It was a rare occasion when the population of London did not stop and stare at Myles Devereux when he arrived, but tonight, they had more pressing worries as they prepared to watch all they owned turned to ash before the day was born.

Seeing the hopelessness of the situation, Myles had no intention of sitting on his horse and watching his money burn. There was nothing that could save the tavern. The fire had too tight a hold. When the flames had taken their fill, all he would be left with was a smouldering pile of ash and tumbled brick.

There would be nothing left.

Not only would the Unicorn be gone, but anything of worth would have been taken with it. All the paraphernalia that made a tavern live would be ash. Trestles, benches, tankards, trenchers and barrels would be gone. Cooking pots cracked and warped by the heat would be useless. Pallets, linen and bedframes in the rooms that had been rented would be incinerated. A few benches and stools had been thrown into the road before the Unicorn, but little else; those who sought to save what was inside looked like they had given up quickly.

Fire left you bereft.

"I'll be at the Hart," Myles growled in Matthew's ear.

"You two, with Master Devereux, the rest stop with me." Matthew waved his arm towards the men behind them.

It was the first time Devereux had ridden through London without his dozen, but right now, they were of more use at the Unicorn. If anything could be done, Myles was confident Matthew would do it.

When Matthew returned, it was light.

Myles was momentarily without words when the other man stepped into his room. His shoulders were slumped, and the bright air of energy that Matthew usually carried with him was gone, along with his red bonnet and leather jerkin. He wore only a stained linen shirt with a cloak around his shoulders; his face was blackened, the wrinkles around his eyes standing out in white comedic lines. And he brought with him the evil smell of the pyre.

"Matthew, are you alright?" Myles said, rising.

Matthew raised a hand, nodded and dropped into one of the chairs near the fire. Myles rounded the desk, slopped wine into a glass and brought it to him. "Here."

Matthew drained it in a single gulp. "The whole row is gone, most of the houses are down, and Mistress Herbert and her two bairns didn't get out."

Herbert was Myles' recently appointed landlord at the Unicorn; Myles asked, "And Herbert?."

"He did, but he's a burn on his back that'll take him to the Lord. He was trying to reach his wife, but they were too far away, in rooms behind the kitchen. There wasn't a chance," Matthew said, then added, "We tried to stop him, but he got by us."

"Christ, anyone else?" Myles asked. If he was held accountable for the deaths, there would be a hefty fine to pay.

Matthew shook his head. "It started in the Unicorn by all accounts, and those in the street had time to get out before it lit the thatches.

"Do we know where it started?" Myles said.

"I don't know, there was a bang, as loud as a thunderclap, some said, and a few minutes later, flames were coming from a window at the top of the front of the Unicorn," Matthew said.

"An explosion? There's not been a storm," Myles said, confused.

"I don't know what it was. Some say they heard it. Two women living above Hartie's fish shop were spinning, saying they saw a huge flash before the flames took hold. They thought it was lightning. It could have just been the sound of the roof collapsing," Matthew said wearily, "either way, it's taken the Unicorn down and the rest of the row with it."

Myles dropped heavily into the chair opposite Matthew, the bottle in his hand; he refilled the other man's glass.

Matthew raised it to his lips, then wiped them with the back of his filthy hand, his eyes meeting Myle's. "There are others who heard the noise. We've spread the word it was lightning.

Myles nodded slowly. "Agere dei."

"Act of God," Matthew said in agreement, holding his empty glass forward in a hand that trembled. "You'll not be called to account by the parish for the damage. It's better this way."

Myles nodded. It was true if the act was attributed to a higher power, then each Londoner was responsible for their loss. But if the fire could be traced to a chimney, an unattended hearth, or a dropped candle or lamp in the Unicorn, then Myles would be responsible for all the damage the flames wrought, and that was when the trouble started. Men would have suddenly lost priceless items to the fire, their families would stand witness to their possessions, and neighbours would testify to them as well. Spinning looms, lutes, weapons, and all manner of chattels would have been consumed in the fire, and the cost of them would be Myles Devereux's to replace.

It was a blow. The Unicorn was his most profitable tavern after the White Hart, and it had been a building of some worth. Timber framed, slab walled and with a new thatched roof, reaching three stories with stabling at the rear for twenty horses. It had provided food, ale and accommodation and now .... and now it was rubble.

Myles caught Matthew's left hand; the skin was contorted and blistered from the kiss of the flames. "Christ, Matthew, that's bad."

Matthew pulled from Myles's grip. "It's not as bad as some got tonight."

It was a rebuke, and Myles knew it. If Myles was thinking of his property, Matthew's mind was on Mistress Herbert and her children. It did little other than to make Myles feel even worse about the evening. Even Matthew was, for the moment, seemingly trying to punish him. And for what? He could hardly have plunged into the burning tavern and helped, could he? What was he supposed to have done? Stood and watched them burn?

Myles groaned. He covered his hands with his eyes, trying to block out an image. But it was too late; it was already in his mind, his brother, the flames feasting

Chance is a Game

upon him, his eyes locked with those of Myles, his body trembling as he fought to bear his pain in silence ....

Myles stood suddenly. Laying a hand on Matthew's shoulder. "Get some sleep. It will be made right. I promise you."

Matthew's burnt hand caught his wrist. His voice when he spoke was raw. "I have your word?"

Myles nodded. "You have my word."

Myles had made a promise, and he would keep it. He had little feeling for those who had died in the fire. The final count had been four souls. Mistress Herbert and her two children and a man, who, overcome by smoke, died in the street later. But Matthew's pain was tangible, and that did break through Myle's Devereux's brittle shell.

Myles didn't go to the Unicorn later that day. He let Matthew provide him with information about what had happened there and what needed to be done. The frame of the building had survived sufficiently so that it could be reinforced, cleared of debris, and refilled with wattle and coated in daub. It was a blessing. To Myles, anyway, the significant cost of any building was the oak for the frame and the labour and carpentry costs to construct it. The shell of the Unicorn needed repairs only.

"Could it be Finch?" Myles said.

"Well, it is a name I've also had in my mind. He's a reason to want to bring down the Unicorn," Matthew replied, "I suppose I'm going to have to talk to Jeriah and see if that shit, Finch, has had the opportunity to."

Myles raised an eyebrow. "Do let me know how he's faring."

"I'm sure he's enjoying purgatory. Do you want me to bring him here?" Matthew asked.

A look of distaste twisted Myles' features. "I'd rather not have my nostrils filled with the stench of the Tower. He's been there for two weeks now; he'll smell like a rotting rat."

Matthew nodded, adjusting the tilt of his new bonnet. "Fair enough. I'll go with the lads next time they take the cart to the Tower."

Myles watched Matthew leave. Bloody Finch! Until recently, a more permanent solution would have been found. Finch would have lived for no more than an hour after leaving Myles' room. But now he had to be careful; his bookkeeper had tied him to Heresy, and the attention of the sheriff was not something he wanted.

CHAPTER SEVEN

Tasker's presence at the White Hart was both unexpected and unwanted. Myles was busy and had more pressing issues, like salvaging and resurrecting the Unicorn.

"Send the shit away," Matthew said, his temper worsened by the pain from the burn and lack of sleep.

Myles shook his head. "No, if I do that, it'll appear the fire has been a wounding blow. Let him wait a little longer and send him up."

Tasker, puffing slightly from walking up the stairs, stepped into Myles' room, his face set in a mask of condolence.

"I am sorry for what happened; I wanted to offer my help; if I could be of any assistance to you, I would be more than happy," Tasker said, palms open.

Myles's eyes were as hard as flint, and his welcoming smile was brittle and brief. "All in hand, Tasker. Indeed, it seems God has served me well; you might be right about his plans.

Tasker's face clouded with confusion. "How so?"

"The Unicorn will rise, and it is an opportunity to expand her business. I'm acquiring extra land in the row, so the Lord has cleared the path for me," Myles said. The statement was a lie, but Tasker wouldn't know that.

"Well, that's good then," Tasker said abruptly. It was apparent this was not what he had wanted to hear.

Myles, a genuine smile flitting onto his lips, continued. "I will willingly share the plans with you; it will strengthen my business, especially in that part of the city, but I have meetings shortly to secure the land. Perhaps we could meet at the Angel?"

"Of course, and I will understand if you cannot continue our negotiations at the moment, I am happy to continue in a week or so," Tasker said, smiling again.

Myles frowned. "On the contrary.

"Oh, well …. I didn't want to trouble …."

"Not at all. Weren't you going to show me the proof of how you proposed to pay for my business?" Myles said.

"Yes, of course. I can arrange that and send word," Tasker said.

Myles moved forward quickly, linked his slim arm through Tasker's weighty one, and steered him towards the door. "You do that. I'll wait for your message."

Matthew, who had been diligently listening at the door, opened it.

Matthew followed Tasker to the door at the top of the stairs and held it open for him; as Tasker stepped out of view, Matthew threw a questioning glance towards Myles.

Myles mouthed – "What else did you want me to do?" before turning his back and closing the door to his room.

He'd lied to Tasker. The thought of turning the Unicorn's devastating loss into a positive had appeared in his mind the moment he saw the false expression of sorrow on Tasker's face. But the more he thought about it, the more it made sense. Even if only to rebuild the Unicorn's stables on a larger scale. One of the Unicorn's main trade rivals was Tasker's respectable and relatively expensive Black Swan tavern. There was no reason why the Unicorn could not rival it. Size had limited it before, but with more stabling and more rooms, the new and rebuilt Unicorn could take on the role of a respectable merchant inn. Myles tapped his fingers on the desk; the more he thought about it, the more appealing it became.

And he'd be able to share his plans with Tasker, plans he had no doubt Tasker would not like.

Which brought him back to Tasker. What, exactly, was the heathenish monk up to? He could hear a voice somewhere in his mind, "tread carefully."

"Oh, I will," Myles whispered quietly in reply; scooping Amica from the desk, he lowered himself into one of the chairs near the fire, smoothing down the black fur and wondering exactly how to secure the deals he would need to buy the land near the Unicorn.

Myles smiled. An act of philanthropy may be required. An act of God had robbed many of them of their homes and businesses, but he could make them offers they were unlikely to refuse to remove themselves from the street. And he could dress the purchases up as an act of benevolence on his part. Not a bad idea. It would placate Matthew as well.

Amica purred.

"You agree as well, do you?" Myles said, resting his head back and closing his eyes. For once, he was not particularly bothered by the myriad of stray black hairs that had become attached to him.

The meeting was to take place in the Black Swan in Newbold Street; it was Tasker's newest acquisition and definitely a brightly plumed feather in his cap. The Black Swan was a large tavern; behind it, two fields provided grazing and stabling for horses. Many who came to London stopped here, and when they did, they parted with coin. It was an Inn with a reputation for respectability; the rooms it rented to travellers were of decent quality, the food good and filling, and the ale wasn't watered down. All of these commodities, of course, commanded a higher price, but it was one travellers were willing to pay for comfortable accommodation in an Inn where they were unlikely to get their purses cut.

Myles Devereux had been slightly annoyed when he found Tasker had purchased it. Why, he had railed at Matthew, hadn't he been made aware that the Tavern was for sale? It would have been a welcome addition and profitable and given him a good foothold in the west of the city.

Where was Tasker getting his information, and where had he obtained his money? Myles was hoping to receive answers to these two questions before the day closed.

He arrived at the Black Swan with his habitual retinue of twelve men. Myles dropped from his horse, casting the unwanted reins to one of his men. Matthew bellowed orders that were immediately obeyed, and Devereux, Matthew at his side and behind him, four of his men, armed, entered the Black Swan.

The main room was large and boasted two large hearths, both well-filled with burning logs, giving a warm welcome as they stepped over the threshold. The Swan boasted leaded windows on the lower floor, and light poured through these; the inn did not have to rely solely on smoky reed lights and stinking oil lamps for illumination. The floor rushes were fresh, the tables pale, scoured and clean, and the benches solid. It made the White Hart look poor in comparison. Myles was in no doubt it had been prepared for his arrival to make the difference between the Hart and the Swan as vivid as possible. Myles' mood soured the moment his polished boots stepped inside the inn.

Tasker, similarly accompanied by his own men, was waiting for him. He rose from the chair and waved a hand in greeting as he approached Myles. Myles couldn't force a smile onto his face this time.

Tasker's fat body was swathed in fresh tailoring. Gone was the gaudy green and the bright yellow. It had been replaced by a doublet of the current fashion, cut from black velvet, and it stopped Myles' progress across the room dead. The doublet Tasker wore was a copy of one Devereux owned, which Drew had made for him about a month ago. He had even considered wearing it today, but the sky was laden with a low grey cloud that threatened rain, and Myles had no intention of getting it soaked.

Tasker grinned. He'd evidently not missed the expression on Myles' face. "It seems we share the same tailor."

"Indeed," Myles said, refusing to be drawn into that line of conversation; taking his eyes from Tasker, he focused momentarily on pulling his gloves from his hands. Holding them out towards Matthew, who took them, Myles quickly glanced in his direction. Matthew's neatly bearded face, topped with a new slanted leather bonnet, wore a scowl of disapproval. Tasker's impudence had been noticed. Master Drew, his tailor, had a very difficult conversation coming shortly.

"Sir, if you would follow me," Tasker gestured towards a door at the back of the Tavern, two of his men flanking it.

Myles followed Tasker, waving at his own men to wait. One of Tasker's men opened the door for their master, and he stepped inside, followed by Devereux. The man to the left of the door outstretched an arm to prevent Matthew from following.

"Master Devereux doesn't go anywhere alone," Matthew said, pushing the arm out of the way and stepping after Myles.

Both of Tasker's men moved quickly to stop him until Tasker stopped them. "It's alright, lads, let him through.

When the door closed behind them, Myles found himself in a solid, windowless room with no other exit. Around the walls were set wooden boxes and coffers, all closed. A small table in the centre of the room held two oil lamps that cast a warming glow around the walls.

"You'll appreciate that this is here temporarily, only to validate my good faith in these negotiations," Tasker said and lifted the lid on one of the coffers; the thick planked oak swivelled on rusted iron hook and pin hinges and banged against the wall, propped open. "Once you are satisfied, this will be removed. As I am sure you can understand, wealth such as this requires a certain security."

Myles' eyes roved over the contents of the coffer. Dusty, jumbled and disordered, but beneath the veil of

Chance is a Game

dirt lurked gold. Cups, plates, candlesticks, chalices, and thuribles on slack chains. Tasker walked around the room triumphantly, lifting each of the lids to reveal their contents, and all were similarly packed with ecclesiastical wealth.

"I would say," Tasker said, beaming broadly, "that this will more than cover the price you gave me."

Myles stooped over one of the coffers; on its edge towards the end was a vast gold charger, its diameter spanning the coffer front to back. Myles took hold of a cold edge; taken by surprise by the weight, his fingers lost their grip as he tried to lift it free, and it banged back against the wooden coffer base. Before Myles could attempt to retrieve it for a second time, Matthew's meaty, scarred hand wrapped around it and hefted it from the chest, laying it flat on the top of the rest of the contents.

"I would think there will be ten pounds of gold in that," Tasker moved across the room to stand next to Myles, folding his arms and smiling.

Myles wiped the top of the plate with his hand, brushing away a layer of fine dust. In the centre, a raised depiction of the virgin, kneeling and holding her child, was given life by the lamp light. Myles's fingers rubbed the edge of the plate; a series of figures, hands clasped in eternal piety, were revealed below the dust.

"The apostles," Tasker explained, "with Peter at the top."

"I think," Matthew said, a reprimand in his voice, "Master Devereux can see that."

"Of course," Tasker said, smiling benevolently. "It is a beautiful piece, and sadly no longer wanted. But still a goodly ten pounds, do you not agree?"

Matthew hefted the plate in his hand. "Maybe six," Matthew corrected coldly, sliding the plate back noisily into the box.

Tasker laughed. "Perhaps, but in this box here, there are another twenty, so I don't think there will be a shortage of weight."

Myles' hand had found a ciborium, its lid missing, and lifted it from the box. It sat on a broad base, and the top of the rim was severely dented, but it was undoubtedly at least two pounds in weight of ecclesiastical gold. Myles replaced it and shuffled through some other items: patens, spoons, smaller plates, chalices, and gold lids that had lost their homes. Picking up a chalice, he held it towards the light; it was badly marked, and half of it seemed to be coated in a thin layer of grey mud. Replacing it, he selected another; the inside was half full of the same fine silt. When he removed his hand, the lamplight showed a grey veneer of dust on his fingers. Myles continued his inspection of the coffers and boxes, Matthew a step behind him.

"So, you have seen that I have the strength to bargain with you. Are you willing to discuss terms?" Tasker said when Myles raised his head from examining the last box.

"Very well, come to the White Hart tomorrow, and we can discuss this in detail. Myles was dusting the fine grey powder from his hands and heading towards the door. "Matthew."

Matthew lowered a lid on the last coffer and followed his master towards the door. Myles stopped before it, and Matthew, reaching forward, knocked on it. A second later, it was opened, and Myles stepped back into the relatively bright light of the tap room.

CHAPTER EIGHT

Back in his room at the White Hart, Myles pulled his gloves from his hands and slapped them down noisily on the desk. Stalking towards the open window, he gazed across a grey London, the sky the colour of the fine dust adhering to Tasker's treasures. There was more in that room than the weight in gold that he had asked for. Myles was feeling decidedly uneasy.

Calling over his shoulder towards Matthew, he said, "get Drew here now."

"You want to talk to Drew? Don't you think there are other matters you need to consider rather than a slight to esteem?" Matthew said, his words a rebuke.

"Just get him," Myles countered.

Matthew, was less sympathetic. "He's done it to annoy you, and it's worked."

"Annoy me! Of course, it's annoyed me. Why wouldn't it?" Myles shot back.

"Look, the fool wants to buy your business; he wants to unsettle you. It's a threat, but it's been made to aid his negotiation. Don't let anger cloud your reasoning, Myles," Matthew said, his voice annoyingly calm.

Myles looked up at that. Matthew rarely ever used his first name.

"It's a game. Play it carefully, and play it to win," Matthew continued, "do not let Tasker outwit you."

Matthew's seriously spoken words were correct. It was a game. If he wanted to win it, then he needed to think clearly. Seeing his clothes on the bloody monk had jabbed at his nerves, as it was meant to do.

"He has sent an arrow towards you where he knows it will hurt the most," Matthew said.

"What do you mean?" Myles asked.

Matthew laughed. "He knows how to annoy you, that's all."

"Where, Matthew, did that shit, Tasker, get that hoard from?"

"It's church wealth, all of it," Matthew replied.

"I know that, and it's been hidden somewhere, I would guess, somewhere damp that flood occasionally, given the amount of silt on it," Myles said, annoyed.

"Perhaps, or it's been buried. The only place it could have come from is when old Hal cleared the monasteries out." Matthew tugged thoughtfully at his short beard.

"Or it was hidden from him to stop them from taking it for the benefit of the royal coffers; it's one or the other," Myles said, pointing towards the open window. "At least we know how Tasker has paid for those two new taverns he has in his possession. When I gave him a price of a thousand pounds, I'd no idea his nest was lined with this much gold."

"You asked him for a thousand pounds?" Matthew said, his eyes wide with shock.

"I did," Myles replied.

"A thousand pounds," Matthew repeated, shaking his head in disbelief, "It's got to be an offer worth considering, surely?"

Myles locked his gaze with Matthew's. "Don't even begin to think about it. Do you know how hard it would be to sell that much church gold?"

"There's got to be ways, surely, it would be an incredible ...."

"Christ! You are thinking about it! I knew I shouldn't have told you," Myles grumbled, dropping to sit in one of the chairs near the fire.

Matthew took the opposite. "Come on, that's an amount of money no man can ignore. You'd be a fool ...."

"I'd be a fool to take it," Myles snapped, interrupting Matthew.

"Why?" Matthew said, a crease in his brow, his arms thrown wide.

Myles leaned towards Matthew. "There were twenty boxes in there, all crammed with gold; you can't sell Church plate, not safely; you might get rid of one or two, but not that much. We can't trade in it; no one will want it; it might as well be tainted in blood for all its worth. Why do you think it's been hidden for so long? Because there was no place to get rid of it or market for it, Tasker thinks I am fool enough to exchange my business in London for his worthless church trinkets. It's even harder to trade than that box I bought from Leggy Dodds, and remember what I gave him for that? A groat. That was all he got."

"There's a good quantity of gems used in the decoration, they've got to be easy to sell, and they can't be traced," Matthew argued.

"True, we could prise off all the rubies and emeralds, but that's not going to get that much, is it? Who do I sell that many to?" Myles said impatiently.

"Come on, there are lots of jewellers in London; it can't be that hard to sell them," Matthew said, sounding exasperated.

"Alright, so I sell the gems, and if they account for a tenth of what I wanted, I'd be surprised, so tell me.

How do I get rid of the gold?" Myles sat back and regarded Matthew with serious eyes. "Go on, tell me?"

"It's obvious. We could melt it down. Then no one could see what it had originally been," Matthew stated bluntly.

"And how does that help?" Myles rose quickly from the chair and stalked across the room. "As church trappings, the gold is dangerous, but even melted, it's still problematic. Who would I sell it to?"

"There has to be a market for it," Matthew continued, not about to be put off.

"I don't want anything to do with it, and that's final. Matthew, your memory is a short one; it's only a few scant months ago there was a warrant for my arrest for Heresy. Do you think I want to be found in possession of a hoard of Church wealth? Stolen Church wealth? Make no mistake, Matthew, I doubt very much I will fare so well a second time around," Myles said with feeling.

"That's my point. London is not the safest place for you; why don't we take what Tasker has to offer and leave England, trade this elsewhere?" Matthew said.

Myles flung his arms wide. "Where? For God's sake, Matthew, France and Spain are Catholic and will not take kindly to us trading in ornaments stolen from their Church."

"What about Holland?" Matthew suggested.

"The Low Countries are as Catholic as Spain and France, and the first scent of stolen goods being sold or bartered without paying dues to the governors, we'll be in a worse position than we are now. In England, we can protect ourselves, to a degree," Myles said, exasperated.

Matthew was not for giving in. "There's Ireland; they are not well disposed to their English overlords."

Myles laughed and threw his arms in the air. "They couldn't scrape together enough coin from their Irish arses to buy that gold. Everything of worth has been bled from them, and don't even bother to mention Scotland to me."

"I wasn't going to ...." Matthew said morosely.

"Good," Myles said with finality. "Besides the simple fact that I cannot understand a word that seeps through their beards, I'd freeze to death before we'd finalised a deal."

Matthew rose, still annoyed. Myles could almost feel the anger emanating from him, realising he needed to placate him, he said. "Look, I'll make some enquiries; if there is a way to sell it safely, I'll consider it. Will that satisfy you?"

"It makes sense, and it's an opportunity. You are blinded by your dislike of Tasker, that's all," Matthew said, and before he could see fury burn Myles' cheeks red, he pulled the door open and left.

"Blinded!" Myles growled and then cursed. He could understand why Matthew wanted to accept the deal, but it was unsettling that the man was throwing sense to the wind. It was not a safe course of action, but for Matthew's sake, he'd appear to be considering it until he could show him exactly why he was right.

There was so much more to this. Surely it couldn't be as simple a fact that Tasker had unearthed a pile of Church chattels overlooked by Wolsey and Henry and was using them to increase his standing in London? Could it be that simple? Myles wanted to believe it, but there was something else, something that was making him uneasy. Tasker had never seemed to possess the ambition to carve himself out a territory and then send his dogs to patrol and defend it. He had been happy to make enough money to keep him in the comfortable condition he possessed when a monk. He liked an orderly life, good food, good wine, women, and enough power to satisfy his feeling of self-importance. He was twice the age of Myles, at least, and none of it added up. Unless this was the effect that a sudden influx of wealth could have? Could gold have fired up the man's ambition?

Drew, summoned to the White Hart, had arrived promptly; Myles Devereux was an important and lucrative client. He was left for two hours in the taproom and then another hour in the room outside Devereux's before he was admitted. Long enough to have considered all the possibilities for the delay. Was Devereux just busy? Or had he been brought here for a transgression relating to his tailoring? When Matthew finally admitted him to Devereux's room, he was already a nervous man, and the situation worsened when Devereux spoke.

"So, Drew, when did you decide to make a fool of me?" Myles Devereux said from where he stood propped against his desk, his hands on the wooden edge, his voice acid.

Drew's eyebrows rose in dismay, and his voice, when he spoke, was a squeak. "Sir, I am at a loss."

"Really?" Myles spat the single word in his direction.

Drew swallowed hard; his fears that had been gathering during the lengthy wait had been recognised, and the colour was draining from his cheeks along with

Chance is a Game

his confidence. "Sir, if I have in some way offended you ...."

"Offended me! You've not offended me, you idiot; you've made a fool out of me. Tell me, Drew, at what point did it seem like a good idea in your ridiculous mind to dress that fat cleric, Tasker, in the same clothes you made for me?" Myles demanded.

Drew's creased face slackened, his mouth dropped open, hands suddenly clenched and white knuckled before him.

"You weighed profit higher than any loyalty you owed your client, didn't you?" Myles growled, then when no reply came, he said. "Answer me, damn you."

"It was .... he said he'd seen my work. That you had told him to seek me out and order the very same, I thought I was acting in accord with your wishes," Drew managed, his voice shaking, his eyes fastened on the floor, watering.

"Did he indeed!" Myles said it wasn't the reply he had expected.

"Yes, Master Devereux. He told me he'd admired the doublet when he had met you at The Angel," Master Drew said weakly.

Myles turned his back on the tailor, his temper rising. He'd thought Drew had foolishly sought to profit from Tasker by providing him with clothes he had designed for Devereux. This act would have been very much against his professional code, and he'd chosen to ignore convention for gold. This was, worryingly, not the case. It was something far worse. Tasker had duped Drew.

"Get out of my sight, Drew," Myles said without looking at the tailor; a moment later, he heard the door close.

Tasker had purposefully sought to emulate Myles Devereux.

Why?

He'd referred to his clothing immediately when they met, telling Myles they shared a tailor. Had it been done as a threat? He wanted to buy Myles' business; was this emulation a statement that he had every intention of taking over Myles' position in London in both presence and style.

Myles ran his hands roughly through his hair. One of the rings on his right hand snagged and yanked a dozen strands from his scalp. Myles cursed. Wrapping his hand around the hairs attached to the ring and tugging, he snapped them free.

Looking towards the window, he met Amica's yellow eyes. "What did I tell you? Don't stray onto another's territory. That fat bastard, Tasker, will get more than a split ear!"

CHAPTER NINE

Myles had no intention of falling into a second trap laid by Tasker. Tasker wanted to view what he would be getting for his gold, and Myles would play along for the moment. However, he had no desire to meet with Tasker again soon; that pleasure he would leave to Matthew. After all, Matthew was keen to conclude a deal with him, so let him suffer his company.

"Take your time, bore the bastard to death, and show him the taverns one by one. He'll be very well aware of which ones I own, and it's no secret which ones are the most profitable, so telling him a few facts he will already know won't harm us," Myles said.

"All of them?" Matthew replied.

"Yes, and make sure he spends an hour or two in each and washes a quantity of ale down his neck as you go. We are playing for time, Matthew, while I find out what the fat shit is up to," Myles said.

"How are you going to do that? I can't help you if I'm shepherding Tasker around the city; it'll take all week if you want him to spend a few hours in each," Matthew said.

"I want it to take even longer; it'll make him think we are taking his offer seriously," Myles replied.

"And we aren't?" Matthew said bluntly.

Myles could see disapproval in Matthew's eyes, so he said. "I need time to find out how to trade in his church trappings, Matthew. So, you provide me with that time, and I will find out how it can be done. Agreed?"

He might have been tempted if it had been gold coins. Matthew was still nervous that the charges of Heresy and Treason that had been brought against Myles only a few months ago might reemerge again, and to be fair, there was good reason to believe that it could happen. Those crimes stuck to a man's name like shit, and it was virtually impossible to remove the connection. It was burned into men's minds and wouldn't be forgotten.

It was Friday again.

His clerk, Peter, had settled himself at his desk and efficiently arranged his pens and ink. When Myles had first met the lad, his clothes had been more repairs than original. But over the last month or so, Myles had noted first some newer boots, then hose, and today Peter had a new cloak, brown wool, with shining buckle fastenings. He'd smiled when he saw him, but then he was reminded of the shit, Tasker, and his new clothes, and a little more of Friday's excitement perished.

Martin Prentice, a blacksmith from Newgate Street, had travelled up Devereux's stairs seeking a loan for more materials and two extra smithies. Proudly, he told Myles that he had been appointed the smithy for a tournament the Duke of Norfolk was planning. It was helpful news. With some enquiry, Myles could uncover the scheduled date and, with a few coins exchanged, secure the right to supply ale for the event. He owned taverns in the city, but more importantly, he owned a brewery at the Bird Tavern, and this one single event would sell as much ale as all his other businesses sold in a month.

Profitable indeed.

As far as Fridays went, it was lucrative and well organised, and by noon, the business for the day was completed. The totals and the full purse proof of a good week. Satisfyingly, the parish had settled their account in full; Crinnion had decided, it seemed, to let the issue of the "children" rest, so along with the news from Prentice, a little sparkle was returning to the day.

Matthew gave the briefest of knocks and appeared around the door.

Myles, with a pen in his hand, was trying to calculate the cost of the fire and see if there was some way to mitigate the loss. He scowled at the unwanted interruption. "Aren't you supposed to be entertaining Tasker?"

"Not this afternoon, he had business of his own to attend to," Matthew added. "This has just arrived."

Myles cast the pen down on the table, his eyes fixed on the letter in Matthew's hand.

"It's from Fitzwarren," Matthew crossed the room holding out a thick sealed letter.

Myles sat back heavily in the chair and held his hand for the letter. "It seems today is one of interruptions. Let's see what this one is."

The outer sheet bore a seal he recognised, a two-headed eagle – God, the man was arrogant. It was a device of his own making, the two birds of prey facing away from each other. Myles broke the seal roughly, scattering wax sherds over the desk. Inside was another sealed letter and a brief one in Fitzwarren's hand. Myles flattened the sheet and read.

> *I am no longer in London, but I have a business that may provide you with a profit. My father is being held in poor conditions by my brother in an attempt to control his property. As you know, he is a man of means, and I imagine you can set a high price on his salvation. More, I would imagine, than the cost of resurrecting a Unicorn!*
>
> *R.F.*

Myles smiled broadly.

Richard Fitzwarren was estranged from his father. Myles had known that the old man favoured his heir, Robert, for years. But it seemed Robert had tired of waiting for the title and had disposed of his father. His father was Lord Fitzwarren, aged he might be, no longer on the Privy Council, no longer at the monarch's right hand, but he was wealthy. If Tasker valued his church trappings at a thousand pounds, Lord Fitzwarren would hold the wealth to buy him a hundred times over, and it wouldn't make a noticeable impression on his estates. He had landholdings that stretched from the south coast as far up as Northumberland and west towards the Marches. As the letter indicated, if he was imprisoned by his son, then the price for his salvation would be .... limitless.

Myles pushed the list of numbers he had been working on aside. The Unicorn could wait. Indeed, everything could wait. Myles broke the seal of the second letter, a letter from Richard to his father, bluntly outlining that Myles Devereux would provide him with an escape should he wish to pay for it. And the issue of any negotiation would be one between himself and Devereux.

"What is it?" Matthew said, trying to read over Myles' shoulder.

"This." Myles flapped Richard Fitzwarren's letter in the air. "Is a true fortune."

Matthew pointed a finger at the letter. "How?"

"Fitzwarren's father has fallen foul of his heir, it seems, and he's given me the opportunity to have him in my debt," Myles said, smiling.

"Why is that worth so much?" Matthew demanded.

"Surely, you know the worth of Richard Fitzwarren's father," Myles replied.

"I do, and I know he's not had his father's favour for years, so how would any scheme he has concocted be profitable to you?" Matthew said.

"William has been imprisoned by his heir, Robert, so he can control his property, and Richard has offered me the opportunity to free him and set my own price for that service," Myles said.

"Where is he? If he's imprisoned, how are you going to secure him? Robert will have him well guarded, and you, mark my words, will end up in the middle of a legal mire," Matthew replied.

"I care not what you think; it is an opportunity I will not let slip through my hands," Myles replied.

"Where is he?"

"Around two days' ride from London, not far. It shouldn't take long," Myles replied.

"You can't leave London, not now? We are in the middle of negotiations with Tasker," Matthew blurted.

"I will be gone for four days, no more, and I am sure you will look after Tasker and keep him entertained," Myles replied.

Matthew had argued vehemently against the scheme, but the more he did, the more firmly Myles refused to bend from his course of action. He had no idea if he could retrieve Fitzwarren's father, none at all, but it was an act of his own choosing and not Matthew's.

Matthew finally left Myles alone. With a lump of pale-yellow cheese in his right hand, Myles broke off small pieces and fed them to the cat on his lap. Amica purred her appreciation between morsels. After the cheese was finished, he dusted the crumbs to the floor and rested his head against the chair, eyes closed, his hands warm in the cat's long fur.

Myles had not thought of Italy for a long time. Not because it was a painful recollection but because his mind concerned itself more with the present than the past. Myles supposed it was Fitzwarren's letter that had reminded him of Venice.

Venice.

Myles' mouth twisted into a bitter smile.

That was where everything had started; it hadn't exactly begun as a favourable experience, but it had ended as one. It was the moment his life changed. Completely.

He'd have been maybe thirteen, known then as Jacob, brother of Andrew, and left in Richard Fitzwarren's care while his brother was away. He had been watching a dice game in the Venice tavern; the winning man, Marco, had tossed him the occasional coin so he could join the game. He'd felt so important. And he'd won some games as well. At the end of the night, with five silver denaros in his purse, he'd felt like a king; his only desire was to show them to his brother, Andrew, when he returned.

Marco had thrown an arm around his shoulders, congratulated him on his luck, and invited him to drink with him and continue the game in his room. His head whirling with success and wine, he had readily agreed. Willingly, he followed Marco into his room, where there had been no dice game and no wine. Instead, he'd found himself pinned to a bed, face down, by a man three times his size and strength, and buggered. He'd screamed, not in terror but from the pain, the noise muffled and hidden by the pillow his face was pressed into.

When Marco finished, he shoved Myles roughly from the bed to the floor. Flopping down on his back and pulling a blanket over his body, Marco almost instantly began to snore.

Marco's belt, still with his knife in the sheath, lay beside Myles. With shaking hands, he had pulled the belt towards him; when he was sure the noise had not disturbed the sleeper, he freed the blade. Myles stood on trembling legs and looked down at him. The rucked blanket disguised precisely where the man's body was, and Myles didn't want to miss. Exposed, though, was a hairy throat.

Both hands, white-knuckled, on the hilt, he'd plunged it into the flesh of his neck. The blade went in, and Marco was dragged, gurgling, from his slumber for one last time, with Myles clinging onto the knife hilt, trying to silence him.

Marco had uttered no words; he was shrieking like a stuck pig with blood spraying from his throat; his hands were over Myles' trying to pull the knife away. He'd managed to wrench it out and turn it on Myles, the blade piercing his skin just below the collarbone.

Fitzwarren had heard the noise and forced his way through the door. He tried to pull them apart. The slippery knife hilt was dragged from Myles, and the blade cut through Fitzwarren's doublet. There was a struggle he could barely remember, flailing arms, hands clutching at the knife, then Fitzwarren, his own blade in his hand, had cut through the bastard's windpipe. The shrieks were reduced to gurgling gasps, and between them, they held him down until his lifeblood let out, and the body went limp beneath their hands.

The disturbance had not gone unnoticed, and soon, they had found themselves under arrest and interred in a pit in the Piombi. They were to be dragged before the officials in the morning to give an accounting of themselves, and the goaler housed them with another Englishman already in their custody.

He had no recollection of the night after they were dragged from the tavern. Fitzwarren told him he knew the man they joined in the cell; he was Myles Devereux, a distant cousin of Edward Devereux's. He'd taken a beating, and there was a fever upon him, and when the bells tolled for prime, he breathed his last. Fitzwarren had swapped his clothes with the unconscious Jacob.

After that, it had been simple, so Fitzwarren had told him. They had a corpse they could hold accountable for the murdered man. Richard could pay his way out of the Piombi; the name Lord Fitzwarren was well known even in Italy, and Jacob was now a cousin of Edward Devereux, thrown in the Piombi for cursing the name of the Doge. A finable, and not a hanging, offence. A fine Fitzwarren had arranged to pay.

He was removed from the Piombi and taken to convalesce in Châteaux Blanc in the Canneregio region of the city, paid for by Fitzwarren. Devereux's servants, of which there were only two, had been unpaid for some time and were more than happy to take the coins Richard provided and leave.

It was three years before he had made his way back to England. The real Myles Devereux's poor mother had died in childbirth, his father followed her to the grave a year later, and there were no siblings. He had been in Italy with only a cleric and a tutor long since turned off. So, Jacob kept the name, and there wasn't anyone to refute his claim to it, and no one ever did, especially after an arranged public greeting by Richard Fitzwarren at a Guild Hall mercers banquet shortly after his return.

The only person who had been unhappy about the deception was his brother, Andrew, but even he had accepted it, eventually. Andrew had felt that what had happened was his fault; he had left him in Fitzwarren's charge while he conducted some business in Venice, so he found it difficult to argue against. Jacob had maintained that it was not as if he was claiming Devereux's wealth or property; all he had taken was a name. And what was the worth of that? Quite a lot as it transpired. But not the kind of value that Andrew would have immediately thought of.

It had all been very expedient, and he'd always wondered if Fitzwarren had hastened the demise of the man they had shared a cell with. He'd always meant to ask him. Myles' mouth twisted into a smile. It was highly probable. Richard was a close friend of his brother, and he'd neglected his duty of safeguarding Jacob. So, if anyone was to blame for the events, it was Fitzwarren.

A dozen men, under orders they would not veer from, arrived at the manor. Capable men, riding good horses with Myles Devereux at their head. Myles dropped from his saddle elegantly, passing the reins to one of his mounted men and waited. Matthew, for once, wasn't with him; he'd left his supervising Tasker. Matthew's right-hand man, Percy, was taking his place.

Three servants had scurried from the yard as they had ridden in, and he was in no doubt that his presence would be quickly reported. Trained eyes told him he was standing in little more than a farm and one lacking money, with broken walls, a hanging shutter, and a yard pock-marked with unfilled holes. As they approached, the fields he had ridden through held poor animals, kept inside walls that spoke of neglect, and the crops were sparse and stunted. This was not an affluent place.

A man, a cudgel in his hand, backed by another similarly equipped, appeared in the central doorway to the building.

"What'll you be wanting?" He called from the top of the steps.

"Lord Fitzwarren. We are here to escort him back to his home in London, under orders from his son," Myles replied, pulling a riding glove from his hand slowly, one finger at a time.

"But I never 'erd anything about that, he never sent word?" The man replied, sounding confused.

"You have word now," Myles said, tucking his gloves into his belt.

Suspicion ran across the man's face slowly like leaking water. "How do I know you're from his son?"

Devereux let out a long sigh, fished inside his doublet and produced a folded sheet of parchment. He didn't offer it but simply held it out. "I would doubt you can read. This is for Lord Fitzwarren from his son, and I am to deliver it."

"Give it here, I'll see he gets it." The man extended a hand but remained at the top of the steps.

Myles shook his head. "No. Take me to him. Now!"

The man took one step back towards the door to the house; the other opened it, and it was clear that they intended to slam it closed in the faces of the men in the yard.

Myles turned his eyes skyward. Then, gesturing towards his armed and mounted men, he said, "Take some sage advice and bring me to Lord Fitzwarren, now."

"I'll have him brung down to you," the man conceded before slamming the door shut.

Myles nodded towards the door and stood back, arms folded, and watched as his men began to force the door and enter the manor. He heard shouts of protest and a woman's high-pitched shriek.

Impassive, he waited.

"Lord Fitzwarren is being brought down now," Percy reported from the doorway. "Would you prefer if we brought him outside? It's not fit for beasts in here."

Myles smiled with satisfaction. "Don't worry, even if I sup with beasts, it doesn't mean I shall become one. I would speak to him alone, ensure that is the case."

Percy, nodding, ducked back through the door, reappearing five minutes later when the necessary arrangements had been made.

Myles entered the hall. His men were spread throughout the occupants. Solid, armed and menacing. He let them lead him towards a door at the end of the meagre hall, opening it for his master to step through.

Myles' expression had been unsettled for the first time that day. What he found on the other side of the door was not the man he thought he would meet. He had expected Lord Fitzwarren, a powerful landowner, Richard Fitzwarren's formidable father, privy councillor, friend of Henry VIII, a man of military prowess and undeniable animal cunning. Instead, he came face to face with a decayed old man, wearing rancid clothing with hollowed cheeks, and he stunk like a midden pit.

Myles, turning on his heels, strode back into the main hall. "Is this a joke?"

Percy, stepped forward. "I'm afraid not. That's his servant there." Percy pointed toward a man standing nervously near the doorway.

Myles fastened his eyes on the servant and quickly approached him. "Are you seriously telling me that the man in that room is Lord Fitzwarren?"

The servant nodded, then said loudly enough for the whole hall to hear. "He has been badly treated since he arrived."

"Badly treated!" Myles repeated, his voice incredulous, and then to the servant. "Can he speak?"

"Yes, yes he can, sir," the servant replied.

Myles turned on his heel and returned to the small room with the wizened man. Closing the door behind him, he observed Richard Fitzwarren's father, who was returning his stare with an equally cool gaze. "Your son sent me."

"Which one?" William Fitzwarren replied the voice hinted at a strength long since gone.

Myles folded his arms. "The one who cares, it would seem."

William's mouth hardened into a bloodless line, and he watched as Myles again produced the sealed letter he had waved in the yard. Myles broke the re-sealed letter, scattering wax among the foul reeds covering the floor. He held the sheet before of William's face.

"They've taken my glasses," William stated bluntly.

"Shall I?" Myles asked, his delicate eyebrows raised.

He received a nod of affirmation from the aged head.

Myles reversed the sheet and cleared his throat. "Let me see. 'Should it please you to do so, I have provided the means for you to be removed back to your house in London, which is again your own. Robert's Steward and his men have been removed, and men are in place to ensure they cannot return. The price of your salvation is a matter of negotiation between yourself and Myles Devereux. Signed, Richard Fitzwarren."

"And your name would be Myles Devereux?" William asked, his voice dry and rasping.

Myles nodded, folding the sheet and replacing it inside his doublet, he said with a degree of sarcasm, "I can see age has not deprived you of your wits, old man."

William's eyes narrowed at the slight.

"Be very careful. You might not like what you see, but I am the light, and I am your divine bloody salvation, so shall we get to the issue that I wish to discuss and you wish to avoid?" Myles replied.

"What's that then?" Fitzwarren's voice croaked.

"How much are you willing to pay me to get you out of this shit hole?" Myles replied, grinning wickedly.

CHAPTER TEN

Myles returned to London feeling like he was making a triumphal progress as he entered the city. The old man, along with his servant, were in a covered wagon drawn by two horses, surrounded by Devereux's men; riding at the head was Myles. Entering the city from the west, they made their way by Tasker's tavern, the Black Swan, Myles casting his eyes over the neat black-and-white building.

Tasker!

It was an issue he had not thought about for several days, so absorbed had he been with locating and retrieving his prize before it was too late. A dead Lord was of little use to anyone, and Myles had every intention of keeping this one as hale and hearty for as long as was possible. One of his men had already ridden ahead to ensure a physician would be waiting for their arrival at Fitzwarren's London house.

Tasker .... Myles cursed silently as the name refused to be banished from his mind. Tomorrow, he would return to the issue of the devious monk. Today was one he wanted to enjoy.

Lord Fitzwarren was delivered to his London house, where a sizeable number of Myles Devereux's men were already residing. The security of his newest asset was of the utmost importance. His son, Robert, had tried to take control of the old man and his property once, and Myles had no intention of letting that happen again. Lord William Fitzwarren now belonged to Myles Devereux, and London would soon know this fact.

Once back in his own room at the White Hart, the impressiveness of Lord Fitzwarren's house returned to his thoughts. The exterior was neat herringbone brickwork, crusted with diamond paned windows, and topped with twisted rising chimneys, and he toyed again for a moment with taking it for himself. It would be opulent and luxurious compared to the White Hart and would make an unequivocal statement about Myles Devereux's status. At the back was extensive stabling; it would possess well-trained servants, delightful furniture and private access to the river.

"Amica, you'd like it; the mice would be fatter and weaned on cheese," Myles said, stroking the pleased cat where she sat on the edge of his bed.

But he knew he couldn't, at least not yet. The White Hart lay at the centre of his territory in London; in terms of control, it was the sensible place to be. Fitzwarren's home was further away and it could mean he would no longer be perceived as in control, and given the current problem of Tasker, that would not be a good idea. He didn't want the monk to set a precedent in terms of challengers.

Myles didn't completely abandon the idea of taking the Fitzwarren house as his own but instead decided to keep it as an option for the future. For the moment, he would put 'his' Lord back in it and see what profit he could extract from that.

Myles' thoughts were stopped abruptly by a tap on the door, followed by the appearance of Matthew's head.

"You're back, then," Matthew said, admitting himself to Myles' room.

Myles smiled and, leaning further back into the chair's comfort, announced. "As Cicero recommended, where can one settle more pleasantly than home? Yes, I'm back."

"And?" Matthew said, ignoring Devereux's amused tone.

"'And,' in this instance, I assume means did I succeed? If it does, then yes, I have my Lord, and I have squirrelled him away, a hoard to be exploited in harder times," Myles replied, delight showing on his face. "You wanted me to fail?"

"I did not wish that. I wanted you to turn your attention to a business you already have rather than involve yourself in some scheme Fitzwarren has thrown to you," Matthew replied.

"You disapprove?" Myles said.

"If it was as valuable an opportunity as you think it is, then why would Richard Fitzwarren not have acted to secure the advantage for himself? Have you asked yourself that question?" Matthew retorted.

"We shall see!" Myles replied, his voice cold. "So, did Tasker miss me while I was away, or did you both manage amply without me?"

Matthew, having made his point, relented. "I didn't make him aware you were absent; there was no need to. He's seen what is on offer; it remains only for you to secure a deal with him."

"Very good," Myles replied.

"And you will meet with him again soon?" Matthew said.

"Of course," Myles reassured.

"And the gold, did you make enquiries regarding trading it?" Matthew said, his gaze fixed on Myles.

"I have, and it does look as if I might have found a buyer for Tasker's illegitimate gold; I should have a firm deal in a week or so," Myles lied smoothly.

A weight slid from Matthew's broad shoulders. "Thank the Lord for that. I am pleased I've not had to suffer Tasker's tiresome company for no reason."

Myles smiled. "Not at all. There are a thousand reasons to put up with him." Then, changing the subject, "Did you accompany the cart to the Tower and find out where Finch is?"

"Finch was there, Jeriah swears he's never let him out of his sight, and Finch is fairly well terrified of Jeriah .... but ...." Matthew shook his head, a thumb and forefinger tugging his beard.

"But what?" Myles demanded.

"I don't know, I just have a feeling they were expecting me," Matthew replied, his eyes meeting Myles'.

"Expecting you?" Myles repeated.

Matthew nodded. "Jeriah didn't query why I was there, and before I'd asked, he assured me that Finch hadn't been out of his sight."

Myles rose, linked his hands behind his back, and paced across the floor towards the window.

"Mind you," Matthew continued, "Jeriah will have heard of what happened to the Unicorn. There's not a soul in London who hasn't, and he'd not want the blame for that coming in his direction. He knows Finch was the landlord and has a grievance against you."

"True," Myles conceded, turning back to face Matthew, and asked. "How was Finch?"

"As you said, stinking like a dead rat, with a face grey as ash and trembling in terror when he was summoned to Jeriah's presence – I actually thought he was going to piss himself," Matthew concluded.

"And Jeriah assured you he'd not let the shit out of his sight?" Myles asked.

Matthew nodded. "He did, and Finch is hardly likely to have escaped from the Tower just to return himself back to Hell, is he?"

"True. There are no men who would wish to spend more than a fleeting moment in Jeriah's presence," Myles said, a smile on his face, then asked. "Was Finch still in possession of both his ears?"

"He was. Maybe Jeriah is growing soft," Matthew replied, then added. "Don't worry. Finch did not look like a man who had received any favours from Jeriah."

"The physician is here," Matthew announced without preamble, a look of disapproval on his face when he noted Myles had picked Amica up.

"Send him up," Myles said, lowering the cat to the floor. There was little to be gained by making the physician he had appointed to care for Lord Fitzwarren wait.

Rising, he waited for the man to be admitted.

"Master Devereux," Ishraq said, smiling. He wore the floppy dark cap of his profession and a black robe that ran to the floor, the hem a little grey with dust, and poking from beneath it, black polished boots. He came recommended, Master Ishraq was originally from Tunis, Nonny used his services, and his methods, whilst not conventional, appeared to work.

"So, how is Lord Fitzwarren?" Myles asked.

"He has been mistreated, he has a number of sores, some have putrefied, and he has been poorly fed as well. I have left balms to be applied, and I will attend to him daily as you requested," Master Ishraq replied in his rich, deep African voice.

"Good. And do you think he will recover?" Myles replied.

"I think he has some time left, yes," Ishraq replied, nodding.

Myles' eyes narrowed. "Time left?"

"Yes, I am afraid Lord Fitzwarren has a cancer, it is beyond help, I am afraid; it makes it painful for him to sit, and I have given his servant, Edwin, a liquor to help with the pain," Ishraq replied.

Myles cursed, turned his back on the physician, and strode towards the open window. Richard Fitzwarren, the shit, had failed to mention that he was retrieving a dying man! Matthew might have been right; damn him

"How long?" Myles asked through gritted teeth.

"It is an impossible question, weeks, months, even a year," the physician replied.

"Weeks!" Myles turned round and glared at Ishraq. "Are you telling me he could be dead by the end of next week?"

"That is an unfortunate possibility," the physician replied.

"But with your care, he may live for longer?" Myles said.

"I cannot say with certainty," Ishraq said sadly.

Chance is a Game

"Does he have his senses?" Myles said he would have to make as much profit from this as quickly as he could.

"Please, sir, if you wish to speak with him, give him a few days to rest and recover," Ishraq advised.

Myles waved a hand towards the door. "Keep me informed of his progress daily; you can leave messages here with Matthew. When you feel he is fit to receive a visit, let me know."

Myles watched him leave. He hoped that Ishraq was just ensuring he was not going to be held responsible should his patient die while in his care. Hopefully, the old bastard would still have a few years of usefulness in him.

The White Hart hadn't provided the welcome he had hoped for. His arrival was not anticipated; while he was at the Fitzwarren house, Percy had failed to send a rider across London to alert the tavern staff of their master's return. So, his room was cold. The fire had been out for several days, and the hastily lit one had failed to banish the cold that had eked into every fibre of the room. The linen on his bed was freezing, the wood of the desk as smooth and chilled as ice, and the chairs near the fire served only to suck the warmth from him rather than provide it.

A northerly wind edged with winter and holding a promise of rain snarled through the narrow streets, its cold fingers exploring gaps beneath doors, cracks in walls and rattling closed shutters. A day that should have drawn to a close in two more hours was being brought to a premature end by a dark, sodden sky that had hidden the sinking sun. Night had arrived early in London. Myles' mood had already been damped by the physician and was worsened by the weather, and he took himself to an early and very cold bed.

Unable to sleep, Myles found himself listening to the sounds of the night. Somewhere above him, the rain was seeping through the roof of the White Hart. Running through a breach in the thatch and gathering annoyingly above his room.

Myles watched a drip of water swell. Firelight catching on the glassy surface. Jewel-like, coloured with orange and gold, it hung from the beam at the end of his bed until some unheard command released it. It fell, mercifully, onto the carpet beyond his bed. The beam was empty for a moment, but as he watched, water began to gather, clinging to the woodwork, until it reached the size of a pea, and it too fell.

There was going to be a pond on the floor. Cursing, Myles flung the covers back, snatched a pewter plate from his desk and, with a naked foot, explored the carpet to find where the drips were landing. The next one that fell, cold and unpleasant, slithered down his cheek. Myles set the plate on the floor, stepped back and examined the beam. Sure enough, another drip was ripening and fell satisfyingly into the middle of the pewter plate.

Myles returned to the warm embrace of his bed, pulling the covers close and shutting his eyes.

Then he realised his mistake.

Chance is a Game

Tap ...... tap ...... tap tap .... Tap .... Tap

Myles cursed. What had fallen silently on the carpet was now an annoying and irregular tap on the plate. Myles groaned and sat up. The weather was winning; he was awake, his feet were cold, and sleep was not to be his tonight.

Myles wrapped a fur-lined robe around his shoulders and began to revive the fire in the hearth, feeding it with fresh wood. Out of the corner of his eye, he saw Amica making her way onto the warm side of the bed he had just vacated.

"You'd curl up on a bloody corpse if it was still warm." Myles scowled at the cat. The animal, ignoring him, busied itself, finding the warmest part of the empty bed.

Tap ..... tap .....

Myles flung two more pieces of wood from the basket forcefully into the hearth, pulled one of the chairs closer to the flames, and seated himself, extending his cold feet towards the fire and pulling the robe tighter around his body.

Tap ..... tap .....

Whether he liked it or not, he was fully awake. Myles watched the flames begin to explore the fresh wood he had added. It was dry, axed quarters of elder, the outer edge still crusted with bark, dried moss and lichen, that crisped and fizzled to the fire's touch.

Realising there was now a warmer perch, the cat dropped silently from the bed and jumped into Myles' lap.

"And Matthew says I am fickle," Myles said, wrapping an arm around Amica and receiving a purr of approval in return.

"I can't think properly, Amica," Myles' fingers ran through the thick black fur, his closed his eyes.

Tasker ....

Bloody Tasker.

That was the problem. The impudent monk was pricking at his nerves like a firebrand. The distraction of leaving London, the thrill of his success, and the thoughts of what he could use Lord Fitzwarren for had temporarily, banished Tasker from his mind. He'd been distracted. When he'd returned to London, Tasker had begun to wind his way back into his mind, like a splinter under his skin that he couldn't pull out, festering.

What to do about Tasker?

Tasker.

Matthew still favoured the deal, and Myles was avoiding discussing it with him.

CHAPTER ELEVEN

Callum Asketh was waiting in the White Hart to see Myles Devereux. He had told Matthew the nature of his business and had been told to wait. Finally, after Matthew deemed the wait a suitable length, he was called up the stairs.

"Wait in here," Matthew said as Callum arrived in the outer room. He disappeared through another door and emerged a moment later, followed by Devereux.

Asketh paled as Devereux's cold gaze ran over him from head to toe.

"Matthew tells me you want to sell your shop?" Myles, pulling the chair from behind the desk where Peter usually sat, lowered himself gracefully into it, crossed his legs at the ankles and regarded Asketh with dark eyes.

"Aye, sir. Not that it's much o' a shop anymore after the explosion," Asketh said.

"You mean the fire?" Myles corrected.

"I were in the street at the time, unloadin' wood, when it 'appened, sir," Asketh said.

"When what happened?" Myles said impatiently.

"The explosion, sir. Knocked me off my feet, I were laid flat on me back in the road, a length of oak across me chest and looking up to the sky an' I saw it wi' my own eyes," Asketh said.

"Saw what?" Myles uncrossed his legs and sat upright, about to rise.

"The explosion, like I said. It lifted the roof off the Unicorn, an' I saw it. As God is ma witness, thatch and timbers rose like a bonnet towards the sky, sir," Asketh threw his arms in the air and looked towards the ceiling as he spoke.

Myles' brow furrowed. "Your shop, it's the cobblers next to the Unicorn?"

"Well, sir, it was, but not now; it's a pile of stone and ash," Asketh replied.

"And you were outside when this happened?" Myles continued.

"Aye, sir, I was. An' if I had been a bit sooner unloadin' I'd a' been inside and I'd not be 'ere now," Asketh said.

"And, in your opinion, what caused it?" Myles asked, his eyes locked on Asketh's face.

Asketh's eyes flicked between Devereux's and Matthew's; he licked his lips. "The lightning, sir."

"Let me put this question to you differently," Myles said slowly. "If it wasn't lightning, which we know it was, what else would you have thought could have caused it?"

Asketh looked confused. "Act of the Lord, sir, is lightning."

"I know that, you fool, but what else would you think could have caused that explosion if it hadn't been?" Myles said, his patience beginning to thin.

"Li .... Lightning ...sir," Asketh stammered.

"You idiot ..." Myles was stopped by Matthew, who held his hand up.

"Master Asketh, is a little uncertain as to why we are asking. We are not concerned that this was anything other than an act of God, but we are interested in this explosion. Can you tell us more about it?" Matthew said, his voice calm, and he lay a gentle hand on Asketh's arm. "There is no need to fear any retribution. We simply want to know what happened."

Asketh, seemingly reassured by Matthew's words and tone, began recounting the evenings events to him. Myles, his arms folded tightly across his chest, was forced to listen to an account of how much good clog wood cost, where he had purchased it, and how it was stacked on his cart before he got to the incident outside the Unicorn.

"I'd taken two pieces o' the oak in and returned for a third. It was one o' the longer pieces, and it had quite a weight to it, but I 'ad it balanced in me arms like this as it were too heavy to get onto me shoulder." Asketh showed how he had carried the wood, close to his chest, his arms wrapped around the length. "Then, like a blast o' the hottest wind I ever felt there was this explosion. I were knocked from me feet, and landed on me back with the beam on top of me."

"And where do you think it came from, exactly?" Matthew asked.

Asketh looked nervous again.

Matthew changed his question slightly. "Where do you think the lightning struck?"

"I'd 'ave to say it must have hit the Unicorn and gone to ground there; this great whoosh came out o' the front, took the door off its hinges and flung it into the street," Asketh said.

"The main door at the front of the tavern?" Matthew pressed.

"Aye, the very same. If I'd not been flat on my back, it'd have cut me in half. Ended up on yon side of street, battered off the front of old Al's carpentry shop and stove the shutters in," Asketh said.

Asketh wanted six pounds for his shop next to the Unicorn but was happy eventually to accept three, and, despite more questions, there seemed little he could add to his account.

"Something is not right," Matthew said when Asketh had left.

"I know, if it was lightning, then there's no reason for the roof to blow off; it was something inside the tavern that caused this," Myles said.

"We've already raked through what is left, and there's nothing to see," Matthew replied.

"You weren't looking for an explosion then, were you? You were just trying to see what the fire had left of the Unicorn," Myles said.

"True, but I'm not sure what we are going to find," Matthew said, sounding doubtful, then added, "We need to tread carefully. We've helped spread the rumour that this was an act of God, we don't want to be seen to be changing that by asking too many questions. If it's not an act of God and the explosion is seen to come from the Unicorn, then you'll be paying for this for years."

Myles ran his hand across his mouth thoughtfully. "We'll take another look at the Unicorn. We can do that easily enough, and it would not be suspicious either, as it's known I am looking to rebuild the tavern."

Chance is a Game

Matthew had men at the remains of the Unicorn; some of the stables had survived, and these were serving as accommodation. There wasn't much of value on the site at first glance, but when you looked a little closer, there was a wealth of building materials, including stone, some brick and unburnt timber. None of these Myles wanted to be carried off, as much as possible would be re-used to save money.

The front wall was intact, as were the ends, the eves pointing blackened and roofless towards the sky; inside was a mass of burnt wood, some that had been part of the upper floor hung down from blackened beams still in place across the building. Anything on the ground floor had been reduced to ash: tables, chairs, stools - all gone.

Myles kicked at a broken flagon just inside the door, blackened with the heat, the pottery crumbled into a hundred pieces. Opposite the front door, a large section of the rear wall was missing. It fitted with Asketh's account; if he had been outside the door and felt the force of the explosion, then the wall behind the door had as well.

Myles kicked around at the floor's contents, but there was little to see save burnt timber and thatch. Ducking through the hole in the back wall, he found himself in the tavern yard facing the row of stables. The cobbles were still littered with debris from the fire.

His boot toed a piece of wood. Unburnt, split in half, it was the leg from a stool. Myles picked it up. It wasn't the fire that had done this. Whatever had happened to the stool was not the result of the flames.

Matthew had seen what he had in his hand and picked up a similarly mangled piece of wood. "This is from a window frame, and that over there is the remains of a barrel. Look at it."

Myles discarded the stool leg and walked towards the barrel. It was smashed into pieces. The iron staves twisted like hemp. Matthew picked up what had once been an end. The wood was splintered, torn and unburnt.

Myles leaned over it. "That's broken from the inside, surely?"

"Maybe," Matthew discarded it and, finding another piece of the barrel, pulled it from the debris. It was a section of two long convex barrel staves, and they were snapped like twigs. "It's broken the wrong way. If the roof came down on this, the barrel would be smashed in over."

Myles cast his eyes around the yard. More jagged, unburnt, splintered sharp sherds of wood lay around them. They must have been thrown outside the Unicorn's walls before the fire took hold. Myles picked up one of the splintered staves. "This isn't right."

"I agree, but it's not something we should share," Matthew warned.

Later, back in Myles' room.

"It could have been a chimney fire. If the heat built up and it's blocked with soot, then they have been known to cause an explosion," Matthew said.

Myles shook his head. "The chimney is in the end wall, and that's still standing."

"True," Matthew accepted. "I think we should consider everything before I follow you down the road. I know you are on. It could still have been lightning. If it struck the Unicorn, then it would be the cause of the explosion Asketh saw."

Myles caught Matthew's gaze. "Stop fooling yourself, Matthew, this wasn't an act of bloody God, and you know it. There wasn't a storm that night."

Matthew shrugged. "It could still have been lightning."

"What? One strike? One single bolt, no others across the city?" Myles said, his voice incredulous.

"It could still have been an act of carelessness by someone in the Unicorn. We don't know," Matthew warned.

"Alright, have it your way, but I don't believe heaven is responsible. Our culprit, I think you'll find, has his feet firmly planted on the ground," Myles said acidly.

"Leave it. What does it matter? As far as Tasker is concerned, it was lightning, and he's all that matters now. If you start asking too many questions and he gets word that the Unicorn was brought down by someone other than the Lord, he might start questioning the deal he has struck with you," Matthew warned.

Myles, about to tell Matthew precisely what he thought of Tasker, kept his counsel.

Finch was the name that kept on crawling back into his mind. Finch had every reason to want to see the Unicorn burn, but he had been in Jeriah's keeping and so not likely to have been complicit in blowing the tavern to pieces. From what Matthew had said, Finch was not enjoying his current existence.

Then there was Tasker.

Why make an offer for a business and then attack it? Why burn down something you were trying to buy and the Unicorn as well? It was one of Myles' more lucrative taverns, and Tasker would know the Unicorn was Myles' most profitable tavern after the White Hart. Matthew had taken him there, shown him the inn and the stabling, and he would have known that it was one of the jewels in Myles Devereux's crown.

But why destroy it? It made no sense.

Could the fire be Bennett's doing? There was a truce in place, or at least there was supposed to be one. Had Bennett broken it?

It didn't seem likely. Both men had a hold over the other, and it had only been weeks since Myles had confronted Bennett. Bennett was many things, but he wasn't a fool. He'd bide his time; to strike at Myles like this so quickly would be foolish – wouldn't it? But then Finch had confessed to selling his ale to Bennett, so Bennett was up to something.

Myles sat back in his chair, a thumb and forefinger tugging at his bottom lip. If it was Bennett, then it meant the fire wasn't an accident, and it probably meant as well that the explosion Asketh had heard had been real enough.

So, what had caused it? How could Bennett have blown the back wall of the Unicorn out? There was only one way Myles could think of.

Black powder.

A barrel filled with it inside the Unicorn, near to the back wall. Perhaps buying the ale from Finch had been a ruse to get his men inside the Unicorn? Buy the barrels from Finch and leave an explosive one in their place?

But how did he get hold of so much black powder? Myles had obtained some for Fitzwarren, and it wasn't easy to come by, so how could Bennett have got hold of more of it than Myles could? Production was strictly controlled, and Myles' sources could only smuggle out small amounts, a purse-full at a time. It would take forever to fill a barrel! Then again, did the barrel have to be full? How much did you need to blow a hole in a wall? Fitzwarren had a small bag and had managed to blow the windows out in the Beauchamp Tower.

Myles drummed his fingers on the desk. Blowing out windows was one thing, but taking down a whole tavern was another. Myles sent a silent curse in Fitzwarren's direction; he wasn't in England, he would have been able to tell him what would have been needed to reduce the Unicorn to rubble and blow Asketh off his feet.

Asketh – Myles smiled bitterly. The man said the roof had lifted like a cap being flung into the air, that again was in keeping with a powder explosion inside the tavern rather than a strike of lightning from above.

It was too neat.

Coincidences were not something to be ignored.

CHAPTER TWELVE

Myles knew the owner of the black powder mill at Rotherhithe, he was one Benton Lee, and from time to time, they had dealings together. The Tower was the only other place in London where black powder was manufactured, and Myles doubted that any of that leaked beyond the fortified walls. Recently, he had supplied a small amount to Fitzwarren, but he kept little in stock.

The irksome powder was known as Eastern Gold. Myles had no idea why it had earned that name. It smelt, it was dangerous and of limited use. The problem was it was a commodity with a certain prestige level. And because of that, Myles Devereux liked it to be known that he could supply it. Not that he ever had many customers for it, and he didn't keep more than a few pounds at once. Occasionally, a bag was requested that could be smuggled into the goal, the guards suitably bribed, and the powder, a mercy, hung around the neck of those to be burnt. The powder ignited when the flames touched the dry leather bag, bringing about a quicker end than burning might.

Chance is a Game

It was allowed; it provided an additional spectacle for the gathered crowd when they were splattered with the brains of the condemned. Myles had tried to send some to his brother, the bribes had been taken, the Eastern Gold delivered, but Mary's officers had decreed that the condemned were to suffer and the leather bag had been ripped from around his brother's neck.

Mercy denied, and Andrew had to endure the total pain of the devouring flames as it stripped his flesh and sent his blood to run, hissing, into the faggots.

Myles' nails bit into the palm of his hand, his eyes screwed tightly shut, a remembered smell in his nostrils, the whole horror of the day of Andrew's death, bright and fierce in his mind.

Stop!

Myles slammed a fist down hard on the table, and then he smashed his knuckles twice on the edge, ripping away skin and bruising bone. Pain was the only thing that stopped the vision in his mind.

Holding the injured hand close, Myles settled his breathing and forced his mind to think again about the explosive powder. Fitzwarren had made it quite clear how dangerous and unpredictable the stuff was, and he had no desire to blast himself to heaven. So Myles kept a small quantity in a sealed box packed in greased sheep's wool. He either bought the powder from Lee or, more usually, from those who worked for him who smuggled it from Lee's mill. From what he knew of it, though, it would have taken a goodly quantity, properly handled, to take out the rear wall of the Unicorn.

Had Lee supplied it?

There was only one way to find out.

Ask.

Or rather, take a roundabout way of placing that question.

Lee's business was profitable and progressive. Black powder during old King Henry's time had been largely imported at enormous cost, but now all that was imported was the saltpetre, a key ingredient in the alchemy of war that England lacked in any significant quantity. Devereux arrived, with his men, at the mill at Rotherhithe unannounced.

Devereux was shown into Lee's office without delay. Lee was around the same age as Myles; he ran his business with brisk efficiency and knew everything about the mill's process and about the men who worked there and about his customers. While Myles would never say he liked Lee, he respected and recognised his ability. His business was profitable, but Lee didn't squander his money on tailoring; attired in good quality merchants' brown, the clothes at least provided some substance to a frame beneath that was spare and wanting for flesh. Lee exuded energy and was never still.

"I would ask what brings you here, but that is fairly obvious," Lee said with a grin, rising from behind his desk and extending a hand towards Devereux. "Good to see you, sir, and how's business?"

"It's good," Myles replied, accepting the offered hand.

"Wine?" Lee had already moved towards a side table where glasses and a decanter sat.

Chance is a Game

Myles was about to shake his head, then, changing his mind, smiled in acceptance of the offer. Lee filled two glasses and handed one to Myles. He didn't reseat himself at the desk but strode across to the window and peered into the yard below. He clanked the glass down suddenly on the sill. A quantity of wine escaped over the edge and slopped to the floor. "Damn those men, I'll be back in a moment."

Myles, who had lowered himself into a chair, his legs crossed, observed Lee scuttle from the room at speed with raised eyebrows. He returned a few minutes later.

"Problems?" Myles enquired mildly.

"Bloody idiots, they are unloading sacks of charcoal and stacking it against the wall in the rain! Can you believe it?" Lee said, exasperated.

"The world, I am afraid, has a surfeit of them," Myles replied, taking a sip of wine. It wasn't pleasant, and lowering his arm, he placed the glass on the floor.

"Don't remind me, some days I think all the fools in the world work for me," Lee lamented, returning to the window. "My God!"

Lee flung open the window, his hands on the ledge, and leaned out. "Not there, you fools, inside."

Lee watched them for a few more minutes, then satisfied, he reversed back into the room. "Idiots and deaf to boot! It's a wonder I make anything at all."

Myles smiled. "You make plenty. At a guess, I would say the appetite for black powder continues?"

"It does, and we are opening a second mill. But it's a huge investment, and the costs are ridiculous," Lee lamented.

"The price of making a profit, I am afraid," Myles replied; he paused for a moment, then said, "I have a customer; he'd like two kegs. It's more than I keep, and I wanted to get a price?"

"That's a lot," Lee said, crossing the room and then pacing back to his desk.

Myles shrugged. "Mine is not to reason why; mine is only to supply."

Lee, smiling, turned and tapped his nose. "I think I've a notion who your customer is."

Myles cast an enquiring gaze over Lee. "Go on."

"Don't worry, Devereux, I'll not poach your business; I get to profit anyway," Lee reassured. "Would it be a careless Duke, by any chance?"

Myles, who had no idea where this conversation was taking him, smiled. "It might. What have you heard?"

"Norfolk has a tournament planned, and half of his supplies were stolen. I'm not surprised. Do you know where he kept them?" Lee said, shaking his head.

"No, I don't," Myles replied.

Lee laughed. "Old Henry used the church at Clerkenwell to store his hunting equipment and tournament pavilions there, and when we delivered the powder, you couldn't move in the rooms at the back of the nave for boar spears and rotting canvas. And the fool has no real guard over it, so I'm not surprised it has gone missing. Norfolk has several pieces of ordnance, and they will be fired during the tournament, so he needs a good quantity on hand. Mind you, he had his agents buy directly from me before, so why's he asking you?" Lee said, sounding confused, his dialogue coming to a sudden halt.

"I'm supplying the ale for the event; I'd mentioned I knew you and was asked if I might get a better price," Myles said. The comment, at least, about the ale, wasn't a lie.

"Will you collect?" Lee asked abruptly.

"Of course," Myles said.

Chance is a Game

"For two kegs, the price is sixteen pounds. And you might want to suggest he finds somewhere more secure to store it next time," Lee said.

Within ten minutes, Myles, his expression stony, was mounted on his horse and left the Rotherhithe mill.

Myles was back in his room an hour later. Norfolk had a missing powder keg; it had been stored at Clerkenwell in the church and he'd place a wager that it had been used to level the Unicorn. Myles raised a glass to his lips, then suddenly stopped. His eyes ran around the room, and he set the wine down slowly.

Where was Amica?

Myles frowned. Where was the cat? Myles slowly forced his mind to unpick the previous hours. Gazing into the flames, his mind slowly reversed through the day. He was woken by the bells of St Bride's; the open shuttered window had shown a cloudy day. Amica had not been asleep on his bed; that was not unusual, though. She'd not been there the night before either. Myles remembered putting two pieces of meat from his meal on the corner of his desk for the cat. Both were still there. If she'd been in the room during his absence, they would have been devoured by the feline.

She'd been missing for a day and a half, maybe even as little as a day. Cats regularly went missing, regularly found more exciting pursuits and strayed. And she wasn't Devereux's cat. He had no idea where she had come from. Maybe she had gone back? Myles discarded that thought. It was doubtful that a cat like Amica would swap a palace for a hovel.

Sam Burnell

CHAPTER THIRTEEN

Mathew knocked on the door. The disturbance was business. Matthew walked in, a sword sheathed in his hand and laid it on Myles' desk.

Myles raised an eyebrow. "Do I need to defend myself now?"

Matthew threw him a withering look. "No, thank God."

Myles pushed himself from the chair, joining Matthew at the desk. He assumed the weapon had been pawned. Matthew always presented anything of significant value or interest to Myles. Myles picked it up, clumsily discarding the scabbard and examined the blade, ignoring Matthew's look of despair.

It showed signs of use and a repair to the steel below the hilt. The pommel had a coat of arms Devereux recognised easily enough; it was the device of Somerset.

"I thought you'd want to see it," Matthew said, folding his arms across his chest, admiring eyes on the sword.

Myles was still turning the blade, holding it out out before him. The weight of the weapon was already forcing the tip towards the floor.

"God's bones! If you are going to hold it, at least hold it properly," Matthew admonished. With a gloved hand under the dipping blade, he lifted it to somewhere near level. "And don't lean forward; that just makes it harder to hold it straight."

Myles adjusted his stance and grip on the hilt, the blade somewhere near horizontal, although not particularly still. There was a candle on the desk, set on the top of a pewter holder, thick, triple wicked, and Myles set his eyes on it. Stepping forward, he directed the tip of the sword towards the wax.

He missed. The blade dipped, and the thrust sent the steel to scrape along the top of the polished oak, scarring the wood and lifting a thick curl of wood from the grain.

Matthew's hand covered his mouth, hiding a smile or worse.

Myles scowled and dumped the sword on the desk with a clatter next to the scabbard. "Is it stolen?"

Matthew shook his head. "It doesn't seem to be; it came from Nonny at the Angel; she took it in payment for a debt at her gaming tables."

"How much did she want?" Myles asked, glancing back at the sword.

"Six Angels," Matthew replied.

It was a fair price, perhaps a little more than he would have liked to pay, but it was never a bad idea to keep on the good side of the owner of the Angel. Nonny knew many people, and if the city had news, you could be sure she would know it first.

"Send the money to her," Myles said, then changing his mind, he added, "Actually, I will take it myself."

Matthew picked the blade up and turned it in his hand. "Whoever lost it will be cursing their luck. The weighting is perfect. Granted, there's been a repair, but you are still beautiful."

"Are you actually talking to it now?" Myles said.

Matthew smiled. "It has a soul of its own."

"Really," Myles said sarcastically. "If that's the case, then flog it to the Devil for twice the price."

Matthew tightened his hand around the hilt, and the sword cut through the air in a smooth move. Myles felt the slight draught at its passing. Neat, level and cleanly done, Matthew severed the top from the candle, cleanly cutting through the wicks.

"That's going to be a bastard to relight now!" Myles observed, looking at the wicks cut flush with the candle wax.

"You've got a good edge," Matthew said to the sword, brushing the leading edge carefully with his thumb.

Myles rolled his eyes. "Let me know when the wedding will be, I'll send flowers."

"What?" Matthew said, hauled back from his reverie.

"I said …. oh never mind," Myles replied. "Get me the money Nonny wants, and I'll take it over. And Norfolk has lost a keg of Eastern gold. See what you can find out."

Matthew's eyes narrowed. "When was this?"

"I'm not sure exactly. Recently I assume, he had it stored at the old church at Clerkenwell," Myles replied.

"And you think that might have caused the fire at the Unicorn?" Matthew said, heavy brows knitting together.

"It can't be discounted, can it?" Myles said.

"Bennett?" Matthew said.

"I don't know," Myles said. "See what you can find out. If we can find the thief, then we might find the culprit."

Matthew nodded, sliding the blade back into the sheath; he offered it to Myles. "Do you want to keep it?"

Knowing Matthew would dearly like the weapon and not feeling well disposed to his opinions on Tasker at the moment, Myles said, "I think I shall."

Myles took the offered blade and watched with some minor satisfaction as Matthew, clearly disappointed, left. Myles abandoned the weapon, standing it against the end of his bedpost. He'd give it to Matthew, but not yet.

The Fitzwarren house was only a slight deviation on his way to the Angel, and Myles had a desire to see for his own eyes how his Lord was faring. The word of the physician, one who was selling his skills for a considerable sum, could not be trusted. William Fitzwarren alive was of value, dead he would be useless.

Myles, slender and sleek as a greyhound, stepped through the door. The smile on his face was asinine, his eyes alive with evil delight. A chair was close to William Fitzwarren's, and Myles dropped into it uninvited. Raising a booted foot to the seat, wrapping his arms around his shin and his chin resting on his knee, he observed William with a dark, unswerving gaze.

"Did your mother teach you no manners!" William growled, his brow furrowed, and the grey bushy eyebrows met above the bridge of his nose.

The smile on Myles' face broadened, satisfied that his entrance had been suitably annoying. "I am a poor creature who did not have the gentle life afforded to your sons."

The old man grunted something unintelligible and cast a glance at a full-length painting of a woman that graced the wall next to the fireplace. Myles' eyes followed the old man's. William Fitzwarren's expression as he gazed at the picture was akin to an apology. Myles smirked, and his languid gaze roved over the painting of the woman.

Seeing a sneer leach onto Myles' face, William reddened with fury. "She's my wife. Not one word against her, do you hear me?"

Myles raised a hand and laughed. "If she'd been here, you might have had something to worry about."

"What do you want?" William said, his wasted hands fastening on the chair arms, his attention back on Myles.

"Entertainment, mostly," Myles said, his voice amused. "You know she reminds me of someone …."

William, his lips pressed hard together, remained silent.

"She's got Richard's arrogance, that's for certain," Myles turned his attention back to William.

William continued to stay silent.

Myles pulled his knee closer to his chest and switched his gaze back to William. "So, tell me about her."

William just glared at his visitor.

Myles's shoulders dropped, and with mock exasperation, he said, "Come on, then tell me about Richard. Why has he left London?"

"There's nothing to tell. I've not seen him for years," William provided.

Myles's eyes opened wide at that. "When he was in London, he didn't come to see you?"

The expression that settled on William's face gave him away.

"Oh dear, he didn't. Shame, you could have thanked him for organising my services," Myles said, then laughed; unwinding himself from the chair, he stood and paced towards the painting. "If it was not for my intervention, you would still be king of the dunghill."

The old man had undoubtedly regained his senses; the physician had earned his pay. Now, the question was what advantage could Myles glean from the situation in addition to the ongoing charges he was making for Lord Fitzwarren's security.

"You've seen my son? Spoken with him?" William asked.

"I've seen them both, old man," Myles said, his eyes alight with evil pleasure.

William couldn't help himself. "When? Tell me?"

Myles exited without a backward glance, leaving William's questions unanswered and the old Lord cursing his departure.

CHAPTER FOURTEEN

Nonny sat opposite Myles, her skirts arranged to perfection, her scent blooming around her, and she smiled. "You are looking well, despite your recent .... problems."

"They were more than problems, madam. But now they are happily resolved, and I am here on other business?" Myles said.

Nonny inclined her head. "Go on, 'ow can I 'elp?"

"One of your clients, Tasker. Do you know him?" Myles said.

"I do. Why do you ask?" Nonny said.

"I wish to find out a little more about Master Tasker, and I thought you or one of your girls might help ...." Myles paused, then fishing inside his doublet, he dropped a purse on the table between them.

One of Nonny's eyebrows, fine, narrow and perfect, rose towards her hairline, lifting the corner of her mouth into a smile. Her pale hand, heavy with rings, drew the purse towards her, pulled at the delicate strings and tipped the coins onto the table. Most landed chinking in a pile, one errant Angel, on edge, wheeled across the table. Neither Myles nor Nonny made any attempt to stop it. It prescribed an arc, heading back towards its companions, then, slowing, settled to the woodwork spinning on the spot, the gold winking in the candlelight.

"Well?" Myles said.

"My dear, it is not the girls who can help you," Nonny drew six of the coins towards her. The rest she swept from the table into her open hand and dropped back into the purse. "These are mine for the sword I sent to Matthew, those you can use to gain what information you can, but I cannot promise anything."

"Who then?" Myles asked.

Nonny smiled. "Master Tasker does come here, but not for the girls. His tastes differ, and he has a particular liking for Perkin."

Myles smiled, leaning forward, his fingers plucked one of the Angels from the purse. "And do you think these would help to persuade Perkin to have my interests at heart next time Tasker is here?"

Nonny shrugged, a diamond and emerald necklace trembling on her chest. "Perkin is, 'how you say, sly, and he's likely to try and profit twice. He's not one whose word you can trust."

"And I am, how you say, riche et persausif," Myles said, smiling.

Nonny laughed brightly. "Perhaps you are right, but remember I did warn you, Perkin is not someone to trust."

"Why do you keep him here then?" Myles asked her.

"He is, for the moment, profitable." Then leaning towards Devereux, she added, "and we both know that will not last. So, until then, I might as well make money where I can. Take some wine; I will fetch him for you later."

Chance is a Game

Myles seated himself at his favoured table at the Angel. Wine and a platter of sweetmeats were silently placed before him. He was purposefully at the back of the room; no one in the Angel could observe Myles Devereux. He had an arrangement with Nonny, and the tables and chairs across the room before him were placed in such a way that nobody would be looking directly at him. It suited him well. It meant he could sit at the Angel anonymously, watch the players at their tables, observe exchanges between merchants and nobles, lawyers and clients, and see who was talking to whom.

Tonight, though, Myles cared little for who was in the room and even less for company. He was waiting only for Nonny to produce Perkin. Clicking his fingers, one of his men stepped closer.

"Find me some cards," Myles instructed without looking up.

A few minutes later, a neat deck was placed before him. Myles picked it up and rifled through them. It was not well shuffled, and with a practised hand, he split and reunited the deck three times. Then, knocking the block of cards on the table, he squared up the deck and began to deal before him a solitary game for one. He lay out three cards next to each other: Jack of Hearts, three of clubs and then the eight of diamonds. Myles' hand stopped in the act of setting down a fourth card, and the corner of his mouth twisted into a smile.

It had been a while. Could he still do it?

Myles stacked the three cards together face up, the Jack at the bottom, and began slowly to place the rest of the deck on top. A five of clubs, six of hearts, queen of hearts …. slowly placing each card on top of the next until the pack lay face up before him topped by an ace of spades.

Picking it up, he turned it over and began to place the cards down slowly, naming each one silently before he turned it over.

Jack of hearts
Three of clubs
Eight of diamonds
Two of spades ……
…… nine of hearts

He was now halfway through the pack. Closing his eyes momentarily, he tried to recall the sequence. What came after the nine of hearts? Smiling Myles opened his eyes and turned over the two of clubs. After this was ….. ?

"Let me save you from your solitary endeavour," a voice interrupted.

Myles ignored it, turning over a four of spades.

"I'm pleased to find you here. We have much to discuss."

Myles refused to look up, and turned over another card, eight of spades.

"I'll order wine," a chair creaked with the weight of the uninvited guest.

Myles' concentration began to desert him - the four of clubs or the three of hearts?

Which was it?

Chance is a Game

The three .... Myles turned over the card and glared at the Jack of Spades, banging the rest of the pack down hard on the table he lifted his gaze to the newcomer. "Tasker, I'd like to say it was a delight."

Tasker laughed. "Nobody comes the Angel to enjoy their own company, surely?"

"Solitude is something to be appreciated," Myles replied, scooping the cards from the table and reuniting the deck.

"I don't play myself, never have. Gambling is the Devil's habit," Tasker said, laying a distasteful gaze on the deck Myles had abandoned on the table between them.

"I was hardly gambling, Tasker," Myles said.

Tasker wagged a finger in the air. "You were playing a game of chance, and chance is a game that the Lord does not approve of," Tasker said, with an air of authority.

"And why is that?" Myles said, his voice bored.

"The Lord has a plan for all living souls. To tarry with chance is to flout his will," Tasker said.

Myles reached over and pulled the deck towards him. "If the Lord has a plan, then he knows what the next card will be, am I right?"

"Of course," Tasker said.

"So the Lord is aware that this card is ..... a three of clubs, agreed?" Myles lifted the top card from the deck and held it up.

"Yes," Tasker's self-assurance wavered, clearly wondering where this was going.

"In that case, it's not a solitary game, is it?" Myles said bitingly, placing the card neatly back on top of the others. "Chance isn't a solitary game; it's a game with God."

A ripple of anger ran over Tasker's face, darkening his swarthy features. It was quickly hidden, but Myles noted it with grim satisfaction.

Tasker smiled, then said good-humouredly, waving a stubby finger towards Myles. "You are trying to vex me, Master Devereux, and I'll not allow it."

"Not at all. Wine?" Myles asked, abandoning the cards on the table.

Tasker nodded, and Myles waved a hand in the air; a moment later, a second glass was filled and placed before Tasker. A meaty hand fastened around the delicate stem, and the monk raised it to his lips, staining them red with the liquid. Myles was for a moment, reminded of Justice Daytrew, but he quickly banished the thought. The only thing Daytrew and Tasker had in common was weight. Tasker was no one's fool, and to think of him as such was dangerous.

"I see Matthew is with you," Tasker waved an arm across the room.

Myles shrugged. A look of indifference on his face.

"I thought you might have enjoyed his company," Tasker continued.

Myles held Tasker's gaze for a moment, his expression icy. "Do you regularly sup with your servants?"

Tasker laughed, glancing in Matthew's direction. "I suppose when you put it like that. I had thought he was more than just a servant."

Myles refused to have his eyes drawn toward Matthew and instead leaned back in the chair, draping an arm over the back. "Why would you think that?"

"He is very knowledgeable of your business. I thought he might have more of an interest," Tasker said.

"He is knowledgeable. I pay him very well to be so. He works for me, Tasker, just remember that," Myles warned.

Tasker raised his pale white empty hands and smiled. "If, and it is still an if, I buy your business, would you part with him?"

Myles leered at Tasker and leaned forward. "And I thought you liked them a little younger. But if Matthew is to your taste, he's yours."

A second flash of anger crossed Tasker's face. "That is not what I meant."

Myles shrugged, and waved a hand absently in Matthew's direction. "Whatever, he's yours if you want him."

Myles, raising his eyes to Tasker's face, watched as the man's expression changed to one of distaste; the monk was looking across the room. A moment later, the scent of summer drifted over his shoulder. Without turning, he said in welcome. "Nonny, a pleasure as always."

"Master Devereux, if you have a moment to spare ...." Nonny left the sentence unfinished.

Myles had risen already, taking a plump powdered hand in his. "All my time is yours, lady, should you ask. Tasker, please excuse me."

Not waiting for a reply, Myles tucked Nonny's arm under his and allowed her to slowly lead him across the room.

Perkin was summoned to Nonny's private rooms, where Myles waited with his hostess. He sauntered in on a breeze of arrogance and indolence. His bright blue eyes roamed the room, slowly travelled over Nonny's guest, and then, nodding to the mistress of the house, he sank, uninvited, into one of the plush exotic chairs draped with foil and cushioned with silk.

"Perkin, you know Master Devereux, of course," Nonny said, beginning to rise, "he has a matter he wishes to discuss with you."

Nonny left the room surrounded by a cloud of invisible self-assurance and perfume and closed the door quietly behind her. The lock snapped shut with a loud click, and the candle flames drifted and arched in the draught.

Perkin adjusted his pose, tilting his head to one side and regarding Myles with a dark, enquiring gaze from beneath hooded lids. His face was delicate and fragile; Myles was reminded of his richly embellished Venetian glasses, a luxury that could so easily be broken. He wore only a shirt, hose and boots, the strings of the shirt loose, the white linen sliding to reveal a narrow shoulder with a thin collarbone and pale cream skin smooth as tomb marble, and Myles suspected the heart beneath was equally as cold.

The six gold coins lay still on the table close to Myles; he'd noted with satisfaction that Perkin had not missed them. "Nonny said you may be able to help with some information I need."

A line, as fine as a spider's thread, appeared between Perkins's dark brows; he obviously hadn't expected information to be the currency he would need to tender to gain the gold. He waved a hand airily, "Perhapth. It muthst be of some interest to you

Chance is a Game

if itth worth thix Angels." Perkin's voice was his only flaw, his speech twisted by a lisp.

"Oh, it is," Myles said, settling back in his chair and crossing his legs at the ankles. "And it's worth a lot more than six Angels."

"Go on," Perkin said.

"Tasker," Myles said the name slowly, watching Perkin closely.

"Tathker? Thedrick Tathker?" Perkin said.

Myles laughed. "I hadn't realised the fat shit was called Cedric. So yes, Cedric Tasker."

Perkin shrugged, the linen sliding a little further from the shoulder. "He cometh here sometimes."

"Don't waste time. I already know you are among his favourites. I just wish to know if you will use your ears on my behalf?" Myles said.

"What do you want to know for thix Angels?" Perkin asked.

"It's more than six Angels, Perkin," Myles paused, then continued. "We both know you'll not be here for long, don't we. We both know how it will end for you. And from the look of your face, just below your eye, I think you've already had a taste of it."

Perkin automatically angled his head so the fine scar, hidden by powder, was turned from Myles.

"It is the way of the world. One of these days, probably very soon, you'll have a choice. You'll get your face carved into a new profile, Nonny won't want you, you'll scare the girls and repulse the customers. So, you'll have two choices. Ply your trade in the dark alleys for groats where no one can see your scars, or you go with the man who gave you them. He'll not care; he'll have his prize, and he can do what he likes with you. Not much of a future, is it?" Myles pronounced.

Some of Perkin's self-assurance had drained into the silk. He sat a little straighter, and his thin hands were tight on the chair arms. Now he knew he had no need to seduce the man before him; Perkin's whole demeanour had changed.

"Who told you what Tathker did to me? Wath it him?" Perkin said accusingly.

Myles shook his head, smiling sadly. "No, it was I have to admit, a lucky guess. But we both know how it will end. You go with him willingly, or he'll ruin your face, so you've no choice. It's a common enough trick."

Perkin swallowed hard and stared at Myles. From this angle, Myles could see the long scar that ran from under the eye to the top of the earlobe. It was fine and heavily disguised; the boy had been lucky. "Why didn't you want to leave here and go with him? He's got money; he might be fat and smell of pig swill, but that's a small price to pay."

Perkin took a long breath in and let it out noisily. Pushing his right sleeve up, he held his arm out for Myles to see. "He ith a violent man, I think in not too many months he would kill me."

Myles looked at the puckered skin on the other man's arm. "Well then, it looks like you do need me."

Chance is a Game

An hour later, Myles was back in the White Hart. With help, he had exited the Angel without seeing Tasker again; he had no wish for more of the fat monk's company. His absence had allowed for servants from the tavern to set a fire, warm his bed and replenish the stocks of wood, so his room was pleasantly warm on his return, but it was not a welcome that was to be extended to him by his bed.

The down bolster that ran over the top of the mattress was rucked, and two attempts to flatten it had failed, and a ridge was pressing uncomfortably into the small of his back. The bolster needed removing and beating again, not something Myles was about to engage in. Instead, he decided to move to the opposite side of the bed. The cold linen sucked the heat from his body as soon as he swapped sides, but the bolster was blessedly flat. From this side, he had a view of the fire, and his eyes flicked down towards the hearth. Flames danced, throwing a pale orange light around the room, but Amica was not in her accustomed spot, sprawled before it, her dark fur absorbing the fire's warmth.

Maybe it was the mouser in the tavern that had driven her away? If Amica had been fool enough to stray into his way again, she may have suffered more than a slice in her ear. Who knew? Myles pounded his pillow into a comfortable shape, pressed his head in to it, and tried not to think about the bloody cat.

The window remained an open invitation for the animal. It was ridiculous, so Matthew regularly told him to have the shutters flung wide open and the fire banked high, trying to banish the cold air that leaked through the open window. But that was how Myles liked it. From as far back as he could remember, he'd not liked to be in a room without an escape; he'd not be able to sleep if there wasn't an open window or door propped ajar. Now, it was just a habit. The White Hart was probably one of the best-guarded buildings in London apart from the Tower. Matthew had men posted around the clock, and there was no need for an escape anymore. But Myles still liked the shutters flung back at night; he awoke often, and the sky, the moving clouds and the dark silhouette of the spire of St Bride's absorbed him in those dark, sleepless hours.

Tonight, there was little to see. No spectacular moon casting light through the clouds. No bright stars in the heavens. Nothing. It was cloudy, and the city was blanketed, all light from above banished. He couldn't even see the spire; the open window was nothing more than a black square, and it opened onto the world was only evident by the occasional waft of cold air that explored the room, brushing his cheek. Spring did not want to arrive this year. Winter, with its cold days and wet skies seemed never-ending.

CHAPTER FIFTEEN

Myles, seated at his desk, back to the window, continued on with the costing of the repairs to the Unicorn. With the payments for the additional land, it was starting to look like a very expensive project. Was it worth it? Could he make back this kind of cost? He tallied the list of figures for a third time, confirming that the total was, annoyingly, correct. The income from the Unicorn had been relatively steady during the year; in general, it brought him a profit of five pounds a week. If the business could be returned to that level, then it would take ten years to repay the costs of resurrecting it.

Ten years!

It was too long. Three would make him impatient, but ten! Myles discarded the pen on the desk and regarded his arithmetic with a sour expression. He'd told Tasker he would rebuild the tavern on a grander scheme, and he was beginning to regret the boast.

A scrabble on the sill behind him disturbed his thoughts; turning he expected to see Amica sitting between the open shutters. He'd set a few small cubes of cheese on the sill to tempt the animal back, but instead, he was met with the glassy eyes of a crow; Myles flapped his arms, cursing at the bird. Issuing a loud caw, the bird snapped one of the cubes into its sharp black beak and retreated, wings draughting the air, retreating from the window – triumphant.

Myles sent another curse toward the crow and then rearranged the remaining three pieces of cheese into a neater line, closing the gap where the crow had stolen one. Behind him, he heard the light knock followed by Matthew's unmistakable footsteps.

Turning, Myles saw Matthew looking as if he were about to say something and then, changing his mind, closed his mouth.

Myles didn't miss Matthew's indecision. "What were you going to say?"

"Nothing," Matthew muttered.

"Go on, spit it out; what sage words of wisdom do you have for me now?" Myles said, his tone annoyed.

"It's nothing serious. All I was going to say is that cats don't usually like cheese; you'd be better with fish if you want to tempt the animal back," Matthew said, pointing to the drying chunks of cheese on the sill.

The colour rose to Myles's face. He'd honestly believed no one had noticed his attempt to lure the cat back or that he was indeed affected by the animal's disappearance.

"Fish …." Myles repeated the word haltingly.

"Aye, fish. The smellier, the better," Matthew reassured, then he said, changing the subject and holding out a small square of paper. "There's a message from the Angel for you."

Myles, reaching forward, took the sliver of parchment. To his relief, Matthew adjusted the bonnet on his head and turned his back on Myles, heading towards the door. Myles waited for a moment before unfolding the neat square; when he did, a tiny burst of an unmistakable perfume reached his nose - the woman had no real need to send a written invitation.

He had asked her to inform him if Fitzwarren returned to the Angel, and from the look of cryptic note, it appeared he had.

"L'ange attends votre plaisir,"

Were the only words penned on the sheet in her flamboyant hand.

Two hours later, suitably dressed in a dark, rich green doublet, the sleeves decorated with rich gold brocade, the cuffs trimmed with intricate lace, Myles crossed the city to the Angel with his men at his back.

Nathaniel opened the door and bowed. "Master Devereux, a pleasure as always, to welcome you to the Angel, sir."

Myles, stepping briskly inside, began pulling the gloves from his hands and asked. "Where's Fitzwarren?"

Nathaniel shook his head. "I'm afraid I've not seen him for several weeks."

Myles tucked the gloves into his belt and advanced along the corridor, saying, "that damned man is never around when needed. Let Nonny know I am here."

"Of course. Your usual table, Master Devereux?" Nathaniel asked, quickly catching up with him.

Myles cast a look of disdain in Nathaniel's direction. "Of course."

"Please, give me a moment. There is another there, but I shall have him moved," Nathaniel said, overtaking Myles.

Myles caught his arm before he could leave. "Another? Who?"

"Err .... Master Tasker," Nathaniel said apologetically.

"Why doesn't that bloody surprise me. No need to move him. I'll do that myself," Myles said, heading towards his table.

Nonny kept the table for his use. No one else sat there. The table was Myles Devereux's, and everyone knew that – everyone, it seemed, apart from Tasker.

Myles tried to force a smile onto his lips, but the result was more of a grimace.

"Master Devereux, are you well?" Tasker said as Devereux approached him.

Tasker didn't rise. He remained securely locked in the seat, which would normally be one Myles would use. He could refuse to join Tasker, join him and take a different seat, or oust Tasker from his chair. Myles took in a lengthy breath and weighed the options. There was no way Myles Devereux was going to publicly defer to Tasker.

And he didn't have to.

"Master Devereux, what a pleasure." It was Nonny's sing-song voice from across the room.

She glided towards Myles, the sails of her silk filled with the breeze of her movement.

"A moment of your time, if I may claim it," Nonny said, extending a hand towards Myles.

"For you, of course," Myles said, taking her hand lightly in his and allowing her to draw him away from Tasker.

Nonny wrapped her arm around Myles' arm, and the pair strolled across the room, Nonny waving to two card players seated near the fire.

"And why, lady, are you removing me from Tasker's presence," Myles asked quietly.

"Because, mon cher, he set out to anger you and has been choosing that chair for the last two nights waiting for you to appear," Nonny replied, leaning her head closer to Myles, smiling as she spoke. "That is why I sent a note. It needed to stop and preferably without you setting your hounds on him."

"And you let him sit there?" Myles replied, his tone a little acid.

"What could I do? If I made him move, he would have made his point, and gossip would have made its way to you. It seemed wiser to let the fool be and to disappoint him, and he is sitting there now wondering whether you will or will not return," Nonny said, squeezing Myles' arm gently.

"Hmmm," Myles replied.

"And now that you have answered my message and arrived, he is not just a fool, but he is a disappointed one, and he will not see you again this evening," Nonny said.

"How so?" Myles asked.

Nonny, smiling, squeezed his arm. "Because he hoped to anger you and to make a fool of you, but instead, he is sitting alone watching us leave. Sup in my rooms tonight. I think it would be better," Nonny said.

"There will be another night," Myles replied.

"I think not. Tasker has failed tonight, and I do not suppose he will do this again. You've had a prior warning now; the element of surprise has been lost," Nonny said, and then she added, "and it would provide you with an opportunity now to publicly humiliate him, so no, I doubt he will do it again."

"Perhaps," Myles agreed, sounding unconvinced.

"He will think of something else," Nonny said.

They had arrived at Nonny's private rooms, and Myles held the door open for his hostess. Following her in, he closed it behind them. "And do you think he will?"

"Undoubtedly. Tasker is playing to win," Nonny said, stepping through the doorway.

"And Fitzwarren, do you know where he is?" Myles asked.

"You will have to wait a long time if you want him; he is beyond these shores, I am afraid," Nonny replied.

"Where now?" Myles asked.

"He is on his way to Milan, so I 'ave heard, with his brother," Nonny replied.

Myles bestowed a cold smile on her. "We both know you treat him like a son, so if you have heard anything, it would be from his lips. What's he going to Milan for?"

Nonny inclined her head and regarded Myles with her brown eyes. "If it is as you say, I shall keep a mother's confidence."

"That man has everyone on a tight leash. I thought you at least would be above his brittle charm," Myles said bitterly.

Nonny smiled. "He holds his friends close not with charm, my dear, but with loyalty. It is a very different kind of tender."

"Loyalty, in my experience, madam, is ethereal and regularly traded for gold," Myles said.

"Well then, just think of how valuable it would be if it could not be bought, traded or undermined. What then?" Nonny said.

Myles let out a noisy breath. "Very well, so you will tell me nothing."

"Your Unicorn, will it rise from the ashes?" Nonny said, changing the subject.

"That is the plan. Perhaps I should rename it when it does. Why do you ask?" Myles said.

Nonny shrugged. "It was an unfortunate event for you."

"Unfortunate," Myles said, his voice rising.

Nonny smiled, reached inside a small purse that hung from her wrist and pulled something out. She placed it on the table between them, her hand still covering it.

"What is it?" Myles said, his eyes meeting hers.

"A puzzle," Nonny said, smiling.

"Go on," Myles replied, not liking how the conversation was going.

Nonny took her hand away, revealing a cherub. The small golden child was chubby, winged and holding a flag inscribed, "espoir."

Myles leaned forward and picked it up. The cherub was solid and heavy; if it was gold, and it did look likely, it would be worth five, maybe even six pounds. The reverse was rough; turning it over a twisted peg, snapped and bent, showed where the golden effigy had been attached to something else.

"The seller thought I would like it," Nonny replied.

Myles' frown deepened. "Why?"

"The 'orrid thing has the French word for 'ope in its fat little 'ands and so he thought I would like it," Nonny said.

Suddenly, Myles knew precisely where the piece had come from. Tasker. It had to have been pulled from one of his church trinkets. Myles picked it up again and viewed it closely. The gold was scratched, and in the creases around the cloth wrapped around the child's fat belly was a dark deposit. Myles ran his nail along the recess, freeing a fine grey dust from where it had been trapped.

"Why show this to me?" A vertical line appeared between Myles' brows.

"I thought you might buy it," Nonny said.

Myles put it down, the gold tapping on the woodwork as the cherub rolled on its side. "It's not to my taste either. How much?"

"Four pounds and ...." Nonny smiled. "I shall tell you where I got it from."

Myles' smile matched hers. "Two, and madam, I already know where it came from."

"Oh. come now, I know it is ugly, but still, it has a charm, does it not?" Nonny said sweetly. "It could be made into a cloak pin quite easily."

"A cloak pin," Myles repeated, shaking his head. "And would you wear it?"

"Certainly not," Nonny laughed, then added, "three and a half, and I'll tell you how I came by it."

"Two," Myles settled back in the chair. "I know where it came from."

"Did he steal it from you?" Nonny asked, smiling.

The smile on Myles' face faltered for a moment. Was he wrong?

Nonny had not missed the doubt that had flickered for a moment only across his face, and she wagged a finger towards him. "I 'ave told Richard as well, overconfidence is a man's folly."

Myles folded his arms. "Go on."

"I cannot wear it. Whoever he stole it from will recognise it. The idiot thought he would secure a good price from me simply because of one word."

"And yet you still have it, so perhaps he was right?" Myles said.

Nonny regarded him squarely for a moment. "Sometimes, mon cher, a profit is not easily recognised."

Myles remained silent, his eyes fixed on the woman. Where this was going, he had no idea; like a

Chance is a Game

hare on the course, every muscle in his body was tensed.

"You need not fret; I am not foolish enough to threaten you, and anyway, you are a friend of Richard's, so I have no wish to either," Nonny smiled, then picked up the cherub. "So, where did you think I got this from?"

"Tasker," Myles replied bluntly.

"I assume you have your reasons for believing this was the origin, and it very well might be," Nonny turned the golden infant in her hand.

"So where, mademoiselle, did you come by it?" Myles said.

Nonny smiled. "I want four pounds for it."

"A fair price, I accept," Myle said, his gaze never breaking from hers.

"Very well, take your prize." Nonny placed the cherub on the table before him. "It was given to a man as payment, but he knew he could not trade it easily. So, he brought it to me, thinking I would be flattered to purchase a French Catholic trinket. The seller was your man."

Myles' right eyebrow raised; the question silently placed.

"The landlord of your doomed Unicorn, Master Finch," Nonny replied.

There was between them a long moment of silence. Nonny smiled and said, "So you see why I advise that overconfidence is a folly?"

Myles' eyes had dropped back to the abandoned cherub with renewed interest, and he retrieved it from the table. "Indeed, I can. Finch, you say. Tell me more?"

"He wanted money, that was all, and felt that I may be a safer buyer than many," Nonny said simply.

"Did he indeed. So, you've had this for a few weeks and just thought to mention it? Why now?" Myles said, a trace of sarcasm in his voice.

Nonny's fine brows raised. "Not at all. I purchased this yesterday."

Matthew crooked a finger towards a boy in the corner of the White Hart sitting on his haunches. As soon as he saw the summons, he was on his bare feet bounding across the tavern; as soon as he arrived, he pulled an evil-smelling leather cap from his greasy hair and bowed low.

"Master," Rogan said.

Matthew was forced to lean down. Rogan was the unspoken leader of the rest of the rat boys by virtue of faster fists and a hardened desire to succeed. He was not amongst the tallest of the lads but was certainly the most vicious. Matthew had even winced when he had set about one of the other boys and bitten a chunk of flesh from the back of his arm, emerging from the fight victorious and with blood pouring from his mouth, proudly spitting out the flesh he'd removed and holding it in his hand like a prize. He wanted to become one of Matthew's men, and Matthew was sure that would become the case if he survived.

"Have you seen Master Devereux's cat?" Matthew whispered in his ear.

Rogan's face creased. "The black un with the cut ear?"

"The black one, yes. Have you seen it?" Matthew repeated.

Rogan shook his head. "Nah, master, not for a few days. You want me to see if we can find it?"

Matthew nodded. Then, extending a hand, he took hold of the boy's shoulder, instantly regretting touching Rogan's greasy plumage. "You keep this between us. Do you understand me?"

Rogan nodded, his eyes wide with glee at the confidence that Matthew had just shared.

Matthew released him, wiping the palm of his hand on the seat of his breeches. "Good. Let me know if you find anything out."

CHAPTER SIXTEEN

The question burning in Myles' mind was how could Finch have been to the Angel when he was supposed to be incarcerated in the Tower, under the watchful eye of Hell's own Jeriah? He wanted to talk to Matthew, but that was not to be. His return to the White Hart was not the one he had anticipated, the news that greeted him was that there had been an accident at his brewery, and that the sheriff's men were there, and so, annoyingly, was Matthew.

The brewery was at the back of the Bird in Hand tavern, a small inn that stood on the banks of Mutton Brook, not far from the Fleet. The tavern was not one of his most lucrative, but the brewery was highly profitable. From there, carts would supply all of his London taverns and other independently owned ones with ale.

Myles, mentally prepared for a confrontation with Matthew and wanting answers to questions, was now in a foul temper. It was another half an hour to the Bird tavern, and Myles took with him his retinue; he didn't see why any of them should have the luxury of being out of a saddle when he was still in one.

Arriving at the tavern, his mood was worsened when he found that Justice Daytrew was in attendance. The short, overweight Justice had recently taken too much delight in pursuing Myles Devereux on a charge of Heresy, and Devereux had yet to exact his revenge for justice's zeal.

"Daytrew, what a delight," Myles Devereux announced, dropping from his horse. One of his men was already on hand to take charge of the unwanted mount. Myles' scanned the scene, but he couldn't locate Matthew.

"Master Devereux …. I had heard you were not in the city?" Daytrew said hesitantly, his pig-like eyes, deeply recessed in his fattened face, fixed warily on Myles.

"I returned a few days ago. So are you going to be accusing me of whatever crime you have unearthed here," Myles said, his voice cold.

"Err …. not at all, Master Devereux. I can only apologise for recent events, I was only acting on the order of the …. sh ….sh …. sheriff," Daytrew stammered.

"I am sure you were," Myles said, his tone accusing.

"Have you heard of what has happened to Master Garstang?" Daytrew said, waving an arm towards the Bird in Hand brewery.

"The news that greeted me at the White Hart was simply that there was an issue at the brewery, and the sheriff's men were here," Myles replied. "So, Daytrew, tell me what has happened to Master Garstang?"

"If you'll follow me …. I'll show you. Your man is already there," Daytrew, obviously not wanting to continue the conversation, had already turned and was waddling towards the brewery entrance.

Myles followed.

Master Garstang was in charge of the brewery, an old man with short grey hair a permanently dour expression who hated beer but possessed the skill to keep the brewery running. He was well paid, and now Myles had obtained the concession to supply ale for the Duke of Norfolk's event; he was confident Master Garstang could create the additional beer needed in time. On the return journey, after extracting Lord Fitzwarren from his private Hell, he'd contemplated the worth of the deal, and it would be considerable.

They ducked through the low doorway to the brewery, Daytrew grunting as he bent over, compressing his stomach. Myles grinned as he followed him. Inside, it was even cooler; the brewery building was of stone construction, and high up small square windows admitted light, but none were at the lower levels. Along the length of the structure, rising from the floor, were the wooden brewing vats; like massive half barrels, they rose to twice the height of a man. Steps ran up to a platform, and from there, the tops of the vats could be viewed.

"You need to go up those," Daytrew pointed to the ladder.

"After you," Myles snarled back.

Daytrew paled and turned towards the steps. He'd evidently not wanted to make the ascent, and Myles stood back. He had no intention of ascending behind the Justice and being killed by the idiots falling bulk when one of the rungs gave way.

Daytrew made slow work of the ascent up the ten or so steps. His weight pressured the soles of his soft leather boots, and the rungs were biting painfully into his feet. Myles watched with satisfaction as the justice suffered through the painful climb. Once he was at the top and clear of the ladder, Myles followed him, arriving quickly and smoothly at Daytrew's side.

"I wish I still had the agility of youth," Daytrew said, smiling weakly.

Chance is a Game

"I fear it is not agility you have lost, Daytrew, but the pounds you have gained," Myles said unkindly, then asked. "So where is Master Garstang?"

Daytrew stepped sideways and then pointed to one of the vats. "He's in there."

"What!"

Matthew was on the platform already standing next to the vat Daytrew had pointed to, his bonnet tucked into his belt, and when he looked in Myles' direction, he saw the worried look on the other man's face.

"Master Garstang has been missing for a few days, and the landlord of the Bird in Hand, fearing the worst, had the lads rake the vats with a bill hook, and they found that," Daytrew pointed to a dark, sodden pile of drapery heaped next to the vat.

"And that is?" Myles said, angrily, in no mood for Daytrew's prevarication.

Daytrew swallowed hard. "It's Master Garstang's cloak, sir. I am told that fumes can hover over the vats, and it seems Garstang has been overcome and …. well …. fallen in."

"Fallen in?" Myles said, astounded. "I can't believe it!"

"It does seem so, sir. He carries out an inspection every Friday night; the door had not been relocked, and his cloak has been found, but as yet, not Master Galveston …. when we drain …."

"Drain what?" Myles said, horror in his voice.

"The landlord has told me we can breach the vat at the bottom and drain it, and then we can see if Master Garstang has fallen it. It does seem likely, sir," Daytrew finished apologetically.

"And what's it got to do with you if some simple-minded brewer has lost his footing and fallen into the vat? Eh?" Myles asked.

"Er… it is a matter of the ale, sir," Daytrew replied, his voice thin and reedy.

"What do you mean 'a matter of the ale'?" Myles parodied Daytrew's slightly nasal tone.

"The matter was reported to the sheriffff, and as I am sure you know, sir, the matter of ale quality is regulated by the justices, and we need to ensure it is …."

"It is what …. ?" Devereux snarled.

"Uncontaminated …." Daytrew squeaked.

Myles glared at Daytrew momentarily before leaning past him and taking a wooden cup from where it sat on the window ledge. He dipped it into the top of the vat and thrust it, dripping, towards Daytrew. "As the justice, and having a responsibility for the quality of my ale, drink this, and you can let me know what you think?"

Daytrew's eyes widened in horror. "Sir, I cannot …. we need to drain…. ahhh."

Daytrew didn't finish. Myles threw the ale in his face and the cup in the vat before turning on his heel and heading towards the ladder, "Deal with this, Matthew. Now."

Myles caught the look of anger on Matthew's face as he stepped onto the ladder and began his descent.

By the time he reached the bottom, he realised his actions hadn't been as sensible as they could have been. But he was annoyed. Garstang was missing. He was about to lose a weeks' worth of ale when the vat was drained. And throwing ale in Daytrew's face had been much better than the first thought that had entered his mind, which was to heave the fat shit in and see if he could swim.

Fuming, Myles Devereux returned to the White Hart.

The day was ruined.

Matthew didn't even bother to knock. He opened the door and strode towards the desk Myles was seated behind; swiping the bonnet from his head, he slapped it down, making papers waft.

"You're annoyed." Myles observed unnecessarily.

"Annoyed!" Matthew said, his eyes wide. "Now, what would make you think that?"

"Daytrew, if you remember, recently tried to arrest me for Heresy," Myles replied.

"At the Sheriff's direction," Matthew snapped back. "When it comes to the brewery, the justices have a power over us, whether you bloody like it or not. Giving Daytrew a soaking to satisfy your childish temper was foolish."

Myles exploded from the chair, fists hammering the desk. "As it happens, I have other matters on my mind, Matthew."

"Like what?" Matthew said, anger still in his voice.

"Why is Finch outside of the Tower? Why is he trading in trinkets? The shit has even been to the Angel," Myles growled.

Matthew's expression froze. "Are you sure?"

"Of course, I'm sure. He had gold to sell and traded it with Nonny. When I went there today, she tried to sell me what she'd brought from him," Myles said.

"When did she buy it? Was it recently?" Matthew questioned.

"Yes, very bloody recently," Myles spat back.

"Are you sure?" Matthew said.

"For God's sake!" Myles fished inside his doublet, produced the small gold cherub, and banged it down on the table between them. "Where do you suppose Finch got that from?"

"God's bones!" Matthew stared at the golden child for a moment before he reached out and picked it up, turning it to examine it.

For Myles, the silence had gone on long enough. "Well?

"It looks ...." Matthew didn't finish.

"Go on," Myles said.

"It's been broken off something; look on the back. The gold is twisted ...."

Myles hammered his fist down on the table. "I don't want a bloody valuation, Matthew."

Matthew opened his hand and let the cherub roll from it back onto the desk. "You think he got this from Tasker?"

Myles' eyes opened wider. "Don't you?"

"It could be," Matthew said slowly.

"What do you mean, it could be? That's been brayed off the side of a thurible or the like and given to Finch," Myles said furiously.

"How do you know it was Finch? You didn't see him, I assume?" Matthew said.

"Nonny knew him," Myles snapped back.

"The word of a whore, and how many times before has she met the landlord of the Unicorn? It could have been anyone! If you are trading in stolen gold, using your name is not usually a good idea?" Matthew said.

Myles' face darkened as he realised Matthew was refusing to recognise the validity of his argument. "It fits together too well. Finch has been paid with Tasker's gold."

Matthew raised his palms towards Myles. "Just stop for a moment. Otherwise, you will join a dozen ends together and have nothing more than a kittling rope."

Myles spoke through clenched teeth. "I want to go to the Tower, strap the bastard to a rack, and turn the wheels myself."

"Myles, this isn't helping!" Matthew said, his voice raised. "Stop! We've got Garstang missing, probably in the bottom of a beer vat, the Unicorn levelled to the ground. If Tasker gets news of this, he's likely to revise his offer!"

Myles stared at Matthew; when he spoke, his voice was incredulous. "What do you mean, revise his offer?"

"Exactly that. Tasker's offered you a good sum, the loss of ...."

Myles cut Matthew off. "For the Lord's sake, Matthew, this is Tasker's doing. He's paid Finch in gold, probably to blow the Unicorn up, he's started using my table at the Angel to annoy me, and there's more than a passing chance he's behind Garstang's disappearance."

Matthew stared at him. "Like I said, a dozen ends make a poor rope. Stop that temper of yours for a moment. The only thing you have to connect Tasker to any of this is the possibility, and remember it's just a possibility that this," Matthew's finger stabbed the golden child, making it roll towards Myles. "Came from Tasker's hoard. It's just as likely that it's been stolen from a house or church, pawned or traded; it's not necessarily from Tasker. Remember Myles, money like this piece of gold knows no owner.

Myles stared open-mouthed at Matthew.

"You are siding with bloody Tasker! You want me to sell to him so much you are blind to what's happening!" Myles said.

"I'm not the one who is blind! Your treatment of Daytrew was foolish, and now you are pointing the finger at Tasker because he sat in your chair and dared to use your bloody tailor?" Matthew's voice boomed with anger.

"It's more than that, Matthew, all the evidence ...."

"Evidence you are twisting to your own ends simply because you don't want to take Tasker's offer." Matthew, determined to have the final word, snatched his bonnet from the desk and strode towards the door. A moment later, it slammed.

Myles glared at the closed door.

What was he more annoyed at? Matthew's words or the fact that the man was right?

Groaning, Myles dropped back into the chair and covered his face with his hands. He couldn't believe Garstang had drowned in his own beer. The man was far too serious and efficient for that to have happened to him – surely?

It seemed he had underestimated Matthew's desire for him to sell to Tasker and leave London as well. The bloody fool. He knew his desire came from good intentions; unfortunately, their basis was rocky and unstable.

Damn, Matthew!

Chance is a Game

What was Finch doing away from Jeriah? That was the question he wanted to answer, and it looked as if he'd have to find out himself. And where the Hell was Gartstang?

CHAPTER SEVENTEEN

A message received at the White Hart from Justice Daytrew answered the question as to Garstang's location. It seemed he had indeed fallen into the vat. Myles, inconvenienced and annoyed, made his way back across London. Now, he not only needed to find Finch, but would also have to find another brewer quickly.

"Master Devereux." Daytrew sounded delighted by Myles' arrival; his nervousness had abandoned him. Daytrew, in possession of news that Myles didn't yet know, had climbed to the top of his mountain of self-importance and was about to begin to preach.

With effort, Myles forced himself to remain silent.

"I was right to have the vat drained; my suspicions after his cloak was retrieved were well founded," Daytrew pronounced, his tone slightly nasal, making the fact that Daytrew had been right even more annoying.

When Myles still refused to speak, Daytrew was forced to continue his one-sided monologue. "I've had your men drain the beer from the vat. It takes quite a while for the level to drop; the size of the drains are not large enough to allow for it to flow faster. As the bells struck for Sect the bottom was breached, but it was not until the bells rang again for None that the contents of the vat came into view. You'll understand, of course, that everything would have sunk. The contents were revealed after three hours, maybe a little longer."

Myles couldn't stand it any longer. "What was revealed, exactly?"

"We found Master Garstang in there." Daytrew pointed towards one of the vats, looking grimly satisfied.

Myles stepped towards the vat, his hands on the wooden rim; he peered into the gloomy interior, the smell of ripe beer and hops rising from the gloop at the bottom.

Myles gawped.

It wasn't empty; ten feet below him were lumps of something that he couldn't at first comprehend, nestling amongst the slurry. Then, his mind realised that the contorted shape he was staring at was an arm and that, at the end, pale, palm up over, and filled with a puddle of part-brewed beer, was a hand. The wrist, pale as pastry, had what looked like a chain link laid across it.

Myles stared. Disbelief and shock had slackened his tightly controlled features.

"I'm afraid so," Daytrew said, his voice a pitch higher than usual, alive with excitement; with evident delight he added, "I can understand your shock; the vats have been hiding this hideous crime from sight. I'm having all of them drained, and I fear that .... well .... we might find more."

Myles looked along the building at the four vats, one empty and another half empty, the contents swishing from a vent at the base into a channel and heading towards the beck. The severed arm was gone from his mind, and Myles' features rapidly reordered themselves into a familiar scowl.

"Stop!" Myles ordered, storming along the wooden platform until he was above a man draining the bottom of the vat. "Seal that breach. Now!"

"But, sir, we must drain them; how else do we find Master Garstang?" Daytrew shuffled along the platform to catch up with Myles.

"Did you hear me!" Myles continued to shout, then swinging towards Daytrew, "Do you know how many barrels are in one of these? Do you? There are twenty, and if you pour more into the river, I will send you the bloody bill. *DO YOU HEAR ME?*"

Daytrew stepped back, caught his heel on the edge of an uneven plank and would have fallen had Matthew not appeared behind the justice and prevented his descent.

Daytrew's arms windmilled in the air, and his chins flapped beneath his mouth as he lost his balance. Matthew, having little choice, jammed a shoulder hard into the justice's back to stop his fall. The move prevented the fat man's collapse but it knocked the wind from his lungs, his arms still flailing, Daytrew gasping and pale, flapped like a necked goose.

Matthew, grunted as he hefted the justice back to his feet.

Daytrew opened his mouth to speak, but all that emerged from between the thick lips was a rattling wheeze as he fought to draw in air to his deprived lungs.

Matthew glared at Myles for a moment. "Justice Daytrew, are you alright? It was fortunate that I was just behind you."

"Otherwise, there would have been another body," Myles muttered, under his breath.

"Yes, yes," Daytrew panted, trying to recover his breath and composure; his face was mottled with red and pinpricks of sweat jewelled his forehead.

"Justice Daytrew. Before you continue emptying Master Devereux's ale into Mutton Brook, perhaps a quick explanation would be appropriate. Don't you think?"

"Of course," Daytrew straightened the cloak that hung from his shoulders and wiped the back of his hand across his forehead. Standing a little straighter and trying to regain his authority over the situation, the lapels of his cloak caught in each hand, he began again. "Master Garstang has, apparently, been missing for some days, as you know, and yesterday his cloak was found. No one seemed to know where he was, then this morning, his, well … part of him … was found on the surface of the vat that's now empty."

Myles looked in horror at the empty vat with the white arm nestling in the muck at the bottom. "Part of him?"

Daytrew nodded. "The lungs, you see, had inflated and brought the body to the surface. There's no telling how long it had been in there."

Confusion was playing havoc with Myles' face. "Where is he then?"

"Over there, under the sacking," Daytrew said, evident distaste in his expression.

Not at all bothered by what he might find beneath the hessian, Matthew leaned down and flipped it back. Beneath was part of Garstang, indeed the main part. A headless torso bereft of arms and legs lay naked on the floor. The arms were cut away neatly at the shoulders, but the legs were missing only from below the knee.

"How do you know it's Garstang?" Myles asked; the body, such as it was, robbed of expression, resembled more a side of meat at a butcher's than Myles' brewer.

"We found his head, sir," Daytrew said weakly and pointed towards where the drenched cloak lay. On top, nestling still inside the net that had retrieved it, pale and open-eyed, was Garstang's head. Myles stared at it, his eyes unable to break from the dead man's. There was no blood leaking from the severed neck, and the rags of flesh around his neck hung down in a wrinkled flap. Submerged in the vat, Garstang's eyes seemed to have absorbed the ale and protruded from his head, browned and bulging. A shudder ran down Myles' back. A head on a spike was one thing; having one in close proximity in your own building was quite another.

"When we drained this vat, there were parts ...." Daytrew hesitated, "Not all of Master Garstang was there, so one of the lads got a fishing net, and that's when we found a foot in that one. Which is why we were draining it."

"My God," said Matthew, his eyes wide.

Myles looked down into the half-empty vat, the dark liquid sending a bitter scent to his nostrils, and he felt his stomach turn. "Empty it."

The man below the platform was still frozen to the spot after taking the force of Myles' tirade and didn't move.

"*EMPTY IT!*" Myles bellowed down to him. The man jumped, and a moment later, the rush of ale swilling back into the stone channel could be heard.

"Does anyone know what happened?" Matthew asked Daytrew.

Daytrew shook his head. "No one seems to know anything, only that he had not been seen for a few days."

Myles, who had his back to Daytrew, turned round suddenly, his voice acid, he said. "Well, I think we can say, without a doubt, it wasn't an accident!"

"Quite," Daytrew replied, his voice high-pitched.

"So what have you found out?" Myles stepped towards Daytrew.

"Nothing, so far," Daytrew admitted.

Myles stalked to the very end of the platform. Behind him, he could hear Matthew exchanging words with Daytrew, and a moment later, he heard the unmistakable sound of creaking wood as Daytrew mounted the steps and made his way back down them.

"I hope the bloody rungs give out!" Myles muttered to himself.

"Are you alright?" Matthew said, walking along the creaking planking behind him.

"Of course I'm not," Myles shot back, cold eyes on Matthew, reminding the other man he was not forgiven for his earlier opinion of Myles' actions. "I've just lost ten pounds of ale, and Garstang won't be making me anymore."

"I think there's a good chance we'll need to empty the other two, so prepare yourself for a higher cost," Matthew said, his voice serious. "Why on earth has someone killed Garstang and then distributed him between the vats?"

Myles was studying the planking. "I don't know .... step back." Myles waved a hand at Matthew. "There's a trail of blood .... there. Can you see it?"

Matthew took two steps back and found the droplets Myles had seen spattered on the dark wood. His eyes followed the trail across the planking towards the wall behind Myles. "There, behind you."

Myles turned and found where Matthew was pointing towards the dark wall at the end of the mezzanine. Stepping nearer, Myles realised the reason it was so dark, not only because the high windows cast hardly any light into the corner but also because the stonework was still slick with blood. And worse, fastened to a window bar was a meat hook, spiked, vicious and empty.

Myles stopped dead. "My God! They hung him on the hook and butchered him here?"

Matthew, next to him, his thumbs tucked into his belt, nodded his head, leaning towards the spiked hook. "The chain for the hook has been linked round the window bars; you can see where the weight on the links has chipped away some of the edges of the stone sill."

Matthew, seemingly unaffected by the horror, lifted the hook from the wall, the links jangling as they were rearranged; the hook itself was a vicious horizontal iron bar with two spikes at either end, attached by a triangular frame to the links that supported it.

"I've never seen the like of it. Why? Why would you kill a man and then do that to him?" Myles said, his hand over his mouth; the smell from the ale, mixed with the tang of the blood, made his stomach complain.

"I don't know, and now is not the time to speak of it," Matthew said gravely, letting the iron fall back against the stonework. "I'll show Daytrew where Garstang was murdered. Go back to the Hart. I don't want him associating you with this, and the fool undoubtedly will."

Myles descended back down the ladder and was surprised to find his progress was slowed by legs that were not quite as solid as those that had carried him up a short while earlier.

Myles, accompanied by his men, left, Matthew, remaining to oversee Daytrew's investigation. Myles returned to the White Hart, and when he opened the door to his room, he found his cat was still not there to welcome him.

Matthew returned two hours later. After Matthew had shown Daytrew the corner where Garstang had been murdered, there had followed a detailed investigation of the rest of the brewery for more clues.

"Did Daytrew find out anything else?" Myles asked when Matthew finally returned.

Matthew sat down in one of the chairs near the fire. "Nothing much. He must have been lured onto the platform, or his murderer found him up there and then butchered him in the corner. The blood has run down the wall, but you can't see it on the lower floor as it is behind one of the vats. His purse must have fallen or been cut from him, and we found several silver coins behind one of the vats close to the wall. They hadn't been there long and must have fallen through the gaps in the wood."

"You think he was murdered for his purse?" Myles said, his voice incredulous.

"I doubt very much that it was a murder for money, but still finding a purse on his victim, the murderer took it," Matthew said.

"So, he's expedient and vicious," Myles replied dryly.

Matthew nodded. "Nobody at the Bird in Hand has seen anything, nobody knows if he had any enemies, he was well-liked and there seems no reason for such an attack. And worse, we've had to empty the final vat; it seems the killer used them all."

"Bloody hell, all four?" Myles threw his arms in the air.

Matthew nodded. "I'm afraid so."

Myles closed his eyes, and his long fingers pressed his temples. "That will mean we have nothing to supply the taverns with. Christ, Matthew, we need to find another source of ale quickly."

"And another brewer," Matthew reminded him.

"And another brewer," Myles conceded, then added sourly, "why did the bastard have to get rid of Garstang in my bloody vats? He could have weighed him and dumped him in the river, found some hungry pigs, dropped him to the bottom of a well, buried him in a pit or even incinerated him in a bread oven .... But no, the shit chose to throw him in the ale vats! When I find out who did this, I will cook him in a bread oven, and I'll not kill him first!"

Matthew tugged at his short beard, his forehead creased with a frown. "There's a man I know who worked at the Unicorn before the fire, and he used to help Garstang; it might be he could take over the brewery."

"Find him then, see if he's up to the job," Myles agreed, then added, "mind you, I have to ask myself how many men will want something produced at my brewery after this? It'll not be long before my beer is called brewer's blood."

Matthew didn't reply.

Myles sent an enquiring gaze towards Matthew. "What's the matter?"

"They are not calling it brewer's blood. It's worse than that; the term I've heard is Garstang's guts," Matthew said quietly.

Myles groaned and rubbed his palms over his face. "No one is going to want to buy it. Even if we brew more, it will be hard to sell."

"I know, and the Bird Tavern is empty tonight as it's known Garstang was missing for a few days, so no one wants that in their cup," Matthew replied.

Sudden horror slackened Myles' features. "What about the White Hart?"

Matthew drew in a long breath, then said. "The same, and the other taverns as well."

Myles' long forefinger stabbed the air. "This isn't an accident, Matthew, this is ruinous. It's emptied every one of my taverns. How much money do you think I'm going to lose?"

Matthew was about to say it hadn't emptied the Unicorn but thought better of it and said instead, "men will forget soon enough and take up their old habits again."

"No, Matthew, they won't. They'll find other places to drink; you can be sure Bennett will be fuelling rumours that I've been serving poison and charging for it," Myles' voice trembled with anger.

"If you can still strike a deal with Tasker, then now is the time," Matthew said, his tone conciliatory.

Myles turned a furious gaze on Matthew. "Tasker, again!"

"See sense! The fire and the murder have nothing to do with each other; why you are tying them all together with Tasker, I have no idea. If he still wants to trade that gold for your business, take it with both hands and be grateful."

Myles opened his mouth, thought better of the comment he was about to make, and changed the subject. "I want to know where Finch is. Why is he not under Jeriah's control? Come on, Matthew, he's got to be involved in this? He's got that gold from somewhere, and who would want to strike at my taverns in revenge more than him? First the Unicorn, and now Garstang." "Alright," Matthew raised his hands in surrender. "I'll go to the Tower tonight. I'm sure Finch is there, and I doubt Jeriah has let him lose. We've no leave to enter, so there's no guarantee I'll get in."

CHAPTER EIGHTEEN

Daytrew, like a confused hound, had too many scents in his nostrils and made the mistake of following one that took him to the White Hart, arriving excited and carrying his news like a fresh kill.

"A methodical enquiry has provided some good information," Daytrew announced. His ballooning sense of self-importance expanded his chest, but it still failed to compete with the girth of his belly.

Myles, Matthew's displeasure still ringing in his ears, forced himself to be civil. "Good news, what have you found out?"

"Well, Master Garstang was seen leaving the Bird in Hand to check the brewery; he did this every Friday night around the same time. The landlord and several of his staff at the tavern have confirmed this. Quite a few men were seated outside; there was a break in the bad weather, and a cockfight that had been arranged for earlier in the week was rescheduled for that night. Apparently, the rain had been so bad that the pit was knee-deep in water, and the birds would have had to swim, so they had to change the date ...."

"Yes, yes .... but Garstang?" Myles interrupted Daytrew's diatribe of drivel.

"Yes, well, Garstang was seen heading towards the brewery around the time the entertainment started.

Several men have confirmed this to be the case," Daytrew said, ignoring Myles' evident rising impatience. "There were three rows of benches around the pit. The landlord told me the benches are usually inside the tavern, but when the cockfights are in progress, they are carried outside for the spectators, and beer is served outside, and the kitchens bring ...."

"It is my tavern, Daytrew. I've a good knowledge already of its workings," Myles growled; any pretence at civility was rapidly disappearing.

"Justice Daytrew is just trying to obtain a full picture of the events that took place," Matthew said quickly, then added, "pray continue, Justice Daytrew."

Daytrew smiled happily at Matthew, and when he continued describing the evening, he addressed him and not Devereux.

"Quite. Well, they normally take place on a Monday, but not this week; as I said, the bad weather we've had has given us so much rain that Mutton Brook breached its banks, and water poured into the pit. The landlord said this was why ...."

"Please, Justice Daytrew, can you get to the point," Myles said through clenched teeth.

Looking a little disappointed, Daytrew continued. "The break in the weather meant the pit had drained of water, and the landlord decided the hold the cockfight on the Friday instead. It was a last-minute decision, so there were men seated outside when Garstang left the inn. There would not have been so many on any other Friday, you see."

"So?" Myles said bluntly.

"So, perhaps our murderer thought he would not be observed. But it turns out this may not have been the case. There were men outside for many hours, and there were at least ten fights that night. The landlord told me they are good for business, and so he likes to make sure they run on as long as possible, that way ...."

"Lord save us, Daytrew. Do I need to remind you again? It's my tavern, and I'm well aware of how much ale a man will buy during a fight," Myles said, his temper threatening to erupt.

"The pit, as you might well know, is bordered on one side by the wall of the Bird Tavern, and the benches were arranged around the other three sides. We have located some of the men seated closest to the road; the landlord knows them, you see. They were the nearest to the brewery door, and two remember Garstang entering the brewery," Daytrew paused in his narrative, ensuring he had his audience's attention before he continued with a note of triumph in his voice. "And neither of them can recall seeing Garstang emerge later on."

Myles just stared at the justice. "Of course, nobody saw him re-emerge. That would have taken a miracle of miracles, as by that point, no doubt, he'd been butchered and tossed into the vats."

"Yes," Daytrew said, tapping his nose. "But now we know for certain that the crime was committed on that very evening."

Myles opened his mouth to say something. Thought better of it and rapidly turned his back on the justice. How much of an idiot was the man!

"We know this. It's a certainty that he entered and never emerged, well at least not in one piece – can I assume that by now Master Garstang is no longer littered around my brewery?" Myles snapped.

The colour rose to Daytrew's face.

"For God's sake, Daytrew! You can't just leave him in there!" Myles' voice rose.

"The sheriff has visited the site, and because of the atrocity of the crime, he wishes for everything to be recorded. You have to appreciate, sir, that this takes time," Daytrew countered.

"I am sure Master Devereux is aware of this and is just impatient for the arrest of whoever is responsible for Master Garstang's murder," Matthew intervened quickly.

Myles turned his back on Daytrew, cursing under his breath as he strode across the room. Daytrew was enjoying this; he was paid by the parish for work he carried out, and the longer he made it last, the more lucrative it would be. So Daytrew would be in no hurry at all to bring this to a swift conclusion. "And meanwhile, Garstang is rotting in my vats; it's not ideal Daytrew. How much longer?"

"Another day or so, and we will be finished. Then the sheriff will review the case," Daytrew said, then changing the narrative, "and we have also found chains in the bottom of one of the vats. They were wound around Master Garstang's midriff to ensure it sank, we assume."

"Chains?" Myles repeated bluntly, remembering the iron links he had seen laid across a pallid wrist.

"Yes, sir. They are iron and believed to have come from the docks," Daytrew said.

"And why do you think this is useful?" Myles said.

"Well, sir, the chains are believed to have come from a ship at the dock, so there may be a connection, and there's more." Daytrew couldn't resist the pause. "We might be able to trace a ship that they belong to and narrow our search for the culprit."

"Did you learn anything else?" Myles snapped back.

"The men at the cockfight, although most were looking in the wrong direction, you understand, some of them did recall seeing a man hurrying from the brewery later that night, and it wasn't Master Garstang," Justice Daytrew said triumphantly.

"Who was it? Did they see him clearly," Myles asked, turning back to face Daytrew.

Daytrew shook his head sadly. "By that time, it was quite dark, so we know only that he was cloaked and was hurrying towards Black Neck Street. If you go down Black Neck Street, it is the shortest route to the river and the docks, and that is where the chains could have come from, so the murderer may have been returning there. We are going to make enquiries there tomorrow."

"Very well, if you learn anything more, let me know." Myles knew that there was little point in continuing this conversation, and he wished to be rid of Daytrew.

"I will, and when a time and date is set for the coroner's inquisition, I will send a message," Daytrew said; then, failing to keep a slight smile from his face, he added, "You will, of course, as Master Garstang's employer, need to attend."

Myles stared at Daytrew for a moment. "The sheriff has ordered an Inquisition by the coroner? Why? The cause of death is fairly evident, and you don't have any suspects? What are the jurors expected to make of that?"

"It is the sheriff's decision, sir, not mine, and if my enquiries go well, we may unearth men at the docks with questions to answer," Daytrew said defensively.

"I hope your enquiries are fruitful, Justice Daytrew, and if you need any help or have any more questions, just send a message," Matthew said; taking Daytrew's arm, he began to steer him towards the door.

Myles watched in silence as Matthew accompanied Daytrew down the stairs, the justice thanking Matthew. The door swung closed, and both men were obscured from view.

Daytrew was looking for a cloaked man of no particular note, who had been seen hurrying towards the river. There was little chance he would find a suspect. How he had been appointed justice was beyond comprehension; one could only assume that he had bought the position. If his superiors had appointed him based on merit, then there was little hope for the parish.

The news of the inquest, however, was more than unwelcome. Enough attention had been attracted by Garstang's demise already; a public enquiry would just make it worse.

Half an hour later, a man was standing in Myles Devereux's presence who had also been present at the rescheduled cockfight – Leggy Dodds.

"No doubt you've heard what has happened at my brewery?" Myles said bluntly.

Leggy, adopting a suitably regretful expression, said, "aye, master, a bad business indeed."

Leggy, his jerkin decorated with plumage, with cock feathers sprouting from his cap and with long legs supporting a thin body, was looking ever more like a bantam.

"Justice Daytrew, have you seen him?" Myles asked.

"He's been asking if I or any of the lads round the cockpit saw anyone leave the brewery," Leggy said, shifting his weight from one foot to the other.

"And did anyone?" Myles said.

"I dunno. I didn't, master, I keep my eyes on the birds when I'm working," Leggy said defensively.

"Did the justice question everyone who'd been there?" Myles asked.

Leggy shrugged. "I doubt it; a lot of the lads who come to wager only come when the fights are on, so unless he knows who to look for, he'll not find many of them."

"Of course, you'll know them, and where to find them?" Myles asked.

Leggy grinned, exposing a crooked row of teeth. "I'm running the birds at the Smith's Arms tonight; there'll be a few there that were at the Bird Tavern that night. I can ask around."

"Do that, and when you've finished, come back here and let me know what you've found out." Myles waved his hand towards the door.

Bowing, his plumage floating around him, Leggy Dodds straightened and stalked towards the door on his quick, thin legs.

Myles watched him leave, and the door swung closed in his wake. What was it Leggy had said? 'A bad business indeed,' had been his words. It was more than that, much more. The actual truth was that it was bad for his business.

Leggy dutifully presented himself later that night. Devereux's men had been told to admit him to their master's room so he was not left to wait in the taproom tonight. Unfortunately, he had little use to tell Myles. His fight had been poorly attended and had run to only two rounds before Leggy, mindful of the need to preserve his birds for an occasion when they could make a decent profit, returned them to their cages. He left his lads to lash the cages to his handcart and trundle them to the cock-masters home while he made his way to the White Hart.

"It was a dire fight at the Smith's Arms tonight; not many o' of the lads there. They were gossiping like fish wives, but none of 'em ad anything useful to say," Leggy said regretfully.

"Dire? How so?" Myles asked.

"There was hardly anyone there; I ran two fights hoping more would come, but they didn't, so I packed the birds up. There was no point in wasting them when there are no coins coming in," Leggy replied.

"The Smith's is usually one of your better venues. What happened?" Myles asked. Something in the back of his mind was already telling him he wouldn't like the answer.

"Like I said, everyone's gossiping and tellin' tales about what 'appened to Master Garstang. It's curiosity, I suppose, and they'd rather spend their money on going to have a gander at what's left of him," Leggy lamented.

"What do you mean," Myles said slowly.

Leggy looked suddenly nervous. "With everyone paying to see the murdered man, there's less left to bet on the birds, and there's fewer people in the tavern than usual."

"Paying to see Garstang?" Myles pronounced the words slowly.

Leggy was silent for a moment, then nervously, he said. "I thought it was your doing, sir. Especially with it being your brewery an' all."

"And this is happening tonight?" Myles asked.

"Yes, sir. It's a groat to go in the brewery, an' another if you want to go up the ladders and see the rest o' him."

"Dear God!" Myles gasped. "You, Leggy, are coming with me."

Matthew, on the trail of Finch, was absent. Myles considered waiting for his return but discarded the idea quickly. If he waited, he may have missed the opportunity to catch whoever was trying to profit from the murder.

Devereux, backed by his entourage, stopped in Black Neck Street. At the end and to the left was his brewery. He had no intention of alerting whoever was charging for entry as to his imminent arrival. On foot, accompanied by Leggy and trailed at a distance by two of his men, Myles Devereux sauntered toward the Bird in Hand tavern and the brewery, his identity hidden by his hood.

Two men were flanking the door to the brewery. Neither was known to Myles. The one on the left, the taller, wore a leather bonnet, the flaps covering his ears, his clothes covered by the full-length cloak drawn close around him against the cold. The other, shorter and stockier, wore a thick leather jerkin, fastened with ties, knee length boots, around his neck a woollen scarf and on his head a bonnet that had been pulled down tight over his ears, its original shape deformed. The details of their faces were stolen by the shadows.

As Myles and Leggy approached, the door between the men opened, and two women emerged, one with a cloth over her mouth; her companion, giggling, was holding a lamp, which she handed to the taller of the men. He leaned towards her said something, and both women laughed loudly. The man to the right pointed down the street, whispered confidentially in the ear of the woman on the right, and a moment later, they set off in the direction he had indicated.

"Come on, then, Leggy. Entertain me," Myles said, nudging the cock master forwards, and they crossed the street towards the brewery.

"I've a gent, 'ere who'd like to see inside," Leggy said when they were within earshot and then, winking at the taller of the two men near the door, added, "and he's no mind to wait."

The two men switched their attention to Myles, cowled and standing slightly behind Leggy. "For yer man, it'll be a shillin', and he can take as long as he wants. We'll not let another soul in."

"A shilling? Come on, lads," Leggy replied. "Don't be taking advantage of my master."

The man on the left, holding the lamp, shrugged. "A shillin' it is," and then, leaning towards Leggy, he said, "'an' if yer master wants to take himself something to remember the evening by, we've got a few of these left, for another shillin'."

The cloaked man held up the lamp, and his companion fished inside his jerkin and then opened his hand. The white enamel of Garstang's teeth glinted in the lamplight; the roots, still bloody, had strings of flesh attached to them.

Myles stepped forward; his eyes fixed on the open palm.

"Two shillin's and ye can take ye time and 'ave yer pick of his teeth." The man leered towards Myles.

Myles raised a gloved hand into the air; the men's greedy eyes were fastened on the decoration of gold thread and emeralds that decorated the soft leather. So much so that they failed to notice the movement across the street behind Myles as his men began to close ranks behind their master.

"Two shillin's sir, and we'll let yer man, 'ere, carry the lamp to guide yer." The cloaked man proffered the lamp towards Leggy.

Myles flipped the hood back from his head and glared at the two men.

Leggy, whose reactions were kept sharp by his daily dealings with fast and agile bantams, caught the lamp as it fell. Garstang's teeth he missed, and they descended, twinkling into the mire.

Myles waited. He made no move to follow either of the men, and he didn't need to. Both made it no more than a few halting running steps before they were stopped by Devereux's men and hauled back before their master.

Myles looked between the pair as they were presented back to him, arms pinioned to their sides and a knife persuasively pressed to their ribs.

"Well?" Myles said, his gaze switching between the two men.

"Justice Daytrew, sir, we was gaurdin' the brewery, sir," the man who had produced the brewer's teeth said quickly.

"Guarding it!" Myles repeated, his eyes cold as ice.

"Yes ... sir .... master," Jerkin stammered.

"And did Justice Daytrew ask you to make a profit while you were at it?" Myles demanded.

Neither man answered quickly enough, and the taller received a hard slap to the face that dislodged his flapping headgear. It slipped forward, obscuring his face and muffling his response.

Myles rolled his eyes and folded his arms.

The man's captor smacked his head for a second time, sending his headgear to join Garstang's teeth. "Answer Master Devereux!"

"We was just gaurdin' the brewery, sir," he said again, a little clearer, and received another hard cuff round the back of the head. Four more of Devereux's men had joined them and were standing behind their master, casting their own disapproving looks upon the pair.

"And making a little profit for yourself at the same time," Myles observed, then to his men, "turn their pockets out."

It was a process that had happened before, and Devereux's men did not doubt their master's intentions. The two captives, wailing and protesting, disappeared for a few minutes behind the backs of Devereux's men. Efficiently, every item of clothing was torn from them and handed to one of their number to check for valuables before being discarded into the mud of the street. In a very short time, the two were shivering, bootless, in their shifts.

"That's all we found, Master Devereux," one of his men said, his open hand towards Devereux. The gloved palm held a smattering of thin silver coins, including two clipped ones and another of Garstang's teeth.

Myles took a quick step towards the shorter of the men, who, yelping in fear, stepped back until the wall behind him prevented any further retreat. "And where, pray tell, were you sending those two women?"

Shaking already from the biting cold of the night, the man's trembling worsened. His reply was not made quickly enough, and his unprotected ribs received a vicious jab from his captor.

"Ahh …. It was the landlord of the Thane's Arms, sir," he offered, through teeth gritted against the sudden pain.

"And …." Myles growled.

"If we gave people a password and sent 'em to the Thane's 'ed give us a farthing for every ten, and they'd get …. Ahhhh …."

"That's enough; let him speak. You can deny him his voice afterwards," Myles advised the man's captor. "And what would they get."

"…. an' they'd get a free cup of ale," the man's words tumbled quickly out.

Myles stood back and regarded the man with a cold stare. "And this word they were to give to the landlord, what was it?"

There was no reply.

Myles stepped back and nodded to his men.

"Stop, please …. master," the taller wailed. "It was Garstang's guts."

Myles glared at them. "Lock them up at the White Hart until I decide what to do with them and put a guard on the brewery."

Before he left, he cast a glance down to where the brewer's teeth had been dropped. There was nothing to see.

Pointing down towards the mud, his eyes on Leggy, he said. "Find them."

Myles didn't feel the chill of the night as he rode back towards the White Hart; his temper was boiling his blood. The Thane's Arms, across the other side of the Fleet, belonged to Garrison Bennett, and the shit was profiting from the death of Garstang. Emptying Devereux's taverns to fill his own.

The bastard.

The tenuous truce between them was being stretched to a point where it might very well snap. Matthew had already told him that the phrase used to describe his ale was Garstang's guts, and it seemed now it was Bennett who had taken delight in spreading the word and profiting from it. Myles had no doubt that the Thane's Arms was benefiting from a sudden increase in trade.

CHAPTER NINETEEN

Myles didn't go to bed after Leggy left. There was pain settling at his temples, and the more he thought about the evening, the worse it got. Matthew had yet to return, and he couldn't consider sleep until he knew Finch's whereabouts. Matthew might believe Finch was under lock, key, and Jeriah's control, but Myles certainly didn't.

Myles recognised the tread of Matthew's boots on the stairs beyond his room, set his wine glass down and met Matthew as he opened the door. "Well?"

Matthew's face was grim. "Finch has gone, last week apparently, disappeared along with that shit, Jeriah. Finch is your man."

"I knew it!" Myles raked his long fingers through his hair. "This is my fault; I should have had the bastard's throat cut."

"If there is blame, then it's mine," Matthew said, "I honestly believed he'd not escape from Jeriah."

Myles hauled open the heavy oak door and stalked back into his room. His head hurt. Finding the glass where he'd left it, he lifted it and poured the contents into his mouth. "Ruin, in all her rags, is the ghost of good intentions. It's not your fault. Do you know where he went?"

Matthew shook his head. "At a guess, after the Unicorn burnt, they paid Garstang a visit, and we know how that ended. It's Jeriah's style; he would have delighted in carving the man into pieces. At least we know one thing?"

"What's that?" Myles' mind was distracted, only half listening to Matthew.

"It's not Tasker. His intentions are at least honest, and what has happened can be explained ...."

"Honest?" Myles managed to stop himself and turned the conversation back to Finch. "So, Finch has somehow persuaded Jeriah to join his cause – why would Jeriah do that? There is only one thing Finch could have that would prise him from the Tower? Money, or the promise of it."

Matthew shook his head. "I don't know. Jeriah doesn't have all his wits; you've met him. He might have been drawn to Finch by the promise of violence."

"Jeriah can obtain enough of that to satisfy even his curdled soul in the Tower?" Myles replied, "Finch traded gold with Nonny, and I suspect he has more than that, enough to brighten even Jeriah's blackened heart."

"We need to ensure that he doesn't do it again; there's plenty of other places they could strike at, and ...." Matthew hesitated momentarily. "Arrange to see Tasker again before Finch and Jeriah can worsen the situation."

"What about catching the curs and feeding them into a bread oven, alive? Why am I supposed to avoid them and have them force my hand?" Myles retorted.

"You're not. You saw the gold. That's not having your hand forced. It's an escape. Soon enough, there will be another Finch, or someone will persuade the sheriff to investigate again, and another charge will be hung around your neck. Finch is out there." Matthew pointed towards the open shutters. "And he wants to strike at you, so be bloody careful."

"Who doesn't! There's going to be a coroner's inquest into Garstang's death. If there is a soul in London didn't know about his demise, there won't be one after that," Myles lamented.

"An inquest," Matthew said, his voice suddenly filled with worry. "When?"

"I don't know, it can't be long, can it?" Myles poured himself another glass and drained it. His temper was threatening to escape, and telling Matthew that he'd made a mistake wouldn't help, no matter how badly he wanted to point this out.

"Daytrew'll be called to provide his evidence at the site of the murder. They'll review the corpse, and make a pronouncement," Matthew said.

"I don't think they'll struggle to see it as other than a murder, do you?" Myles said, a third-filled glass in his hand, his tone laden with sarcasm.

"Yes, but whose door will they lay it at?" Matthew replied seriously.

"Daytrew has nothing to connect this to me, nothing at all, Matthew. I'll not be forced to treat with Tasker," Myles' anger was forcing itself towards the surface, and as he raised the glass, wine slopped over the rim.

Matthew's face was stony; he looked for a moment as if he was about to retaliate but instead turned on his heel and left, hauling the door closed behind him.

Myles raised the glass in a toast towards the retreating man. "Bloody fool!"

Myles couldn't sleep. Indeed, he didn't want to. He was very aware that events were beginning to overtake him, and if he didn't take steps quickly, he was sure they would. The only advantage left to him were these dark hours before daybreak. Hauling a bed cloak around his shoulders and forcing his feet into fur slippers, he seated himself before the open window. Briskly, he cleared the desk before him of accounts and bills, replacing them with a clean sheet of vellum, and, next to it, a pen and ink. Perhaps Matthew was right; maybe it was time to meet with Tasker again.

When dawn sent a pale, cold light through the open window, the sheet had been sliced neatly into five. On each section, a different message, now neatly folded and sealed. One for Tasker, one for Daytrew, another for his tailor, Drew, one destined for the Angel, and the last for Garrison Bennett.

Standing at the top of the stairs, Myles shouted into the still-sleeping tavern. "Rogan, get your arse up here, now."

From the corner of the room, a shabby bundle of rags erupted and darted for the stairs, making its way rapidly up the steps.

Rogan stood before Myles with a greasy hat clasped to his chest, head bent, eyes on his bare feet. "Master."

"Look at me," Myles commanded; he held up a coin and twisted it through his long fingers as the boy watched. "This is yours, but first, I've a task for you. I want these delivered, and I don't want you tattling to anyone about this. Do you understand?"

Rogan nodded his head ferociously.

"Good, the first one is to Tasker. Make sure it's delivered to him directly at the Black Swan. Then come back here, and I'll give you the next."

Myles handed the white square to Rogan and wondered for a moment what soiled condition it would arrive in after having been tucked inside the boy's rags. It was a minor annoyance he'd have to live with today. By the time the bells struck for Sect, all the notes had been delivered, and Rogan was back for his payment and the next task Myles had for him and his rat boys.

Matthew's cheeks were puffed and red with fury when he burst into Myles' room unannounced. "You've got two of Daytrew's men under lock and key? Are you bloody mad? The justice has just arrived here, and he's cursing your name."

Daytrew had answered the summons delivered by Rogan just before noon. A little tardy, in Myles' opinion, he was sure if the justice had known the subject of the meeting, he would have arrived sooner.

Myles, dressed in sleek black, rose slowly from behind the desk and raised a finger to silence Matthew. "He's here because I summoned him; any other reason is secondary and will not even be relevant very soon."

"What have you done?" Matthew growled.

"Send the fat wastrel up. I'd like a word with Justice Daytrew," Myles stated bluntly. While waiting for Matthew to return with Daytrew, he pondered how uncomfortable he should make it for the sheriff's underling. Very, or just slightly? Or complicit? Myles grinned.

Myles listened to the steps, complaining as Justice Daytrew hefted his weight up from the taproom. Myles opened the door to his room and greeted him with a smile. Fine lines of perspiration were gathering in the creases of flesh on Daytrew's face and neck, and rising from a collar that looked overly tight was a purple plume that had reached his ears and cheeks. Daytrew did not look well.

"Master Devereux, I have to object most strongly to your removal of my men from their positions last night," Daytrew said, puffing.

"Do you," Myles said, still smiling. "And why would that be?"

"Sir, I understand this is your brewery, but whilst this investigation continues, it falls under my control. When this is reported to the sheriff, he is likely to view it as an attempt to tamper with the evidence, or worse, throw the hounds a fresh scent," Daytrew said with the conviction of the wronged.

"Come into my room, Daytrew; I've something to show you," Myles turned his back on the justice, pushed the door open, and then hitched himself onto the end of his desk while the sheriff's man shuffled in, followed by Matthew.

"Sir, I am not staying. I want you to restore my men's liberty, and I wish to report this matter to the sheriff," Daytrew continued to complain.

"They are your men?" Myles asked.

"Indeed, they are, given my orders to remain outside and guard the brewery," Daytrew replied.

"Just that, guard the brewery, nothing else?" Myles replied, pushing himself a little further back onto the desk.

Confusion rippled Daytrew's face. "I don't understand, sir."

"Oh, you will in a moment, Daytrew. I have below a little court of my own assembling; they should be ready for us about now," Myles dropped from the desk and strode towards the door. "Come on, Daytrew, if you wish to claim your men."

When they descended the stairs again into the taproom, it held half a dozen men and two women. Daytrew's guards, blue with cold, huddled near the fire in soiled linen; two women sat immobile on a bench, their eager eyes watching the room carefully. With his arms folded and leaning against the wall, his plumage floating around him was Leggy Dodds. Seated at a table to his right was Peter, Devereux's clerk, and set before him was paper, and in his hand, ready, a pen poised above an ink pot. Next to Peter, looking uneasy with his current surroundings and fidgeting with the hem of his cloak, was the Parish Clerk, Crinnion.

"What are you doing?" Matthew hissed in Myles' ear.

Myles' long fingers fastened themselves into Matthew's arm. "Anything I want."

Smiling, Myles released his arm and sauntered across the taproom. He scooped a stool from the floor and set it down next to another, looking around at the assembled group. "Justice Daytrew, join me if you will."

Daytrew hesitated and then joined Devereux, his hands on his knees and grunting as he lowered himself onto the stool. Myles couldn't hide the smile that slipped onto his face as the small wooden seat became hidden from view, impaled in Daytrew's rump.

Dragging his attention away from his companion's discomfort, Myles surveyed those in the taproom.

"So, those two are your men? The guards you employed to ensure the security of the brewery and Master Garstang's remains?" Myles said, a long forefinger pointing towards the shivering, nervous men warming themselves by the fire.

"What have you done to them?" Daytrew turned on Myles.

"I've peeled them a little, that's all. Now, are they your men?" Myles said, a malicious smile twitching at the corner of his mouth.

"Of course they are," Daytrew blustered. "Why have you deprived them of their clothes? This is outrageous, Master Devereux."

"And their names are?" Myles asked, ignoring Daytrew's outburst.

"Aertha Merstake and Jake Kidstowe. I object, Master Devereux, to whatever it is you are trying to do here; you have no right to detain my men or myself," Daytrew said and started to extract himself from the stool.

Myles lay a restraining hand on his shoulder. "A few moments of your time, and I am sure all will be clearer. Did you get those names down, Peter?"

"Aye, sir," Peter replied from across the room.

"Good. So, I assume you left Merstake and Kidstowe on guard; they are answerable to you for their actions?" Myles continued.

"They are my men, and they've been treated shamefully," Daytrew continued to object.

"We will see about that," Myles said.

"Where are their clothes?" Daytrew continued.

"I don't think clothing will be an issue for much longer, Justice Daytrew. You have, of course, spoken to Master Dodds during your enquiries?" Myles gestured to where Leggy stood.

"Indeed, but I don't see what this has ...."

Myles raised a hand. "Clarity will be but a matter of a moment. Master Dodds, have you seen these men before?"

"I 'ave, sir, they were gaurdin' the brewery door," Leggy provided.

"And what were they at?" Myles asked.

"For anyone who'd pay them, they'd admit them to the brewery to view the murdered man," Leggy said loudly, with a voice used to addressing a crowd.

"This is absurd," Daytrew exploded, "He's your man, he'll say as you bid him to."

"I'm sure you would think so. So I'll put the same question to Mistress Kent and her daughter." Myles turned to the two women. "Mistress Kent, would you like to tell Justice Daytrew how much you paid for admittance to my brewery last night?"

Mistress Kent straightened her back, swallowed, cleared her throat and began. "I were charged a fathin', master, to go into the brewery an' for the loan of the lamp."

"And what did you see when you were in there?" Myles continued.

"The man who'd been murdered, well bit's o' him." Mistress Kent flushed.

Myles folded his arms, a frown creasing his forehead. "That's very interesting, don't you think, Justice Daytrew?"

"I'm not listening to the words of a gutter whore from Southwalk! She'll say what you want for a coin." Daytrew, his hands on his knees, rocked his body backover with the clear intent of gathering the required momentum to plant his feet on the ground and rise from the stool.

"I understand your concerns, Justice Daytrew, although in Mistress Kent's defence, I do rather think I should point out she works for Thomas Argent as a needlewoman and her daughter as a buttoner. I've also brought Master Tadwell from the Thane's arms to comment. Master Tadwell, would you care to tell Justice Daytrew about your dealings with Merstake and Kidstowe?" Myles said.

Master Tadwell, the landlord of the Thane's Arms, was used to addressing a crowded room, and his voice was easily heard. "Marstake approached me." Tadwell pointed towards the shorter of the two shivering men. "And asked if I'd be interested in paying him if he sent some extra trade my way. It sounded a little irregular, but I agreed. These are, sir, as you can understand, hard times, so he said a farthing for every ten who ordered ale from the tavern."

Myles feigned confusion for a moment. "And how would you know if Merstake and Kidstowe had them sent them your way?"

Chance is a Game

"That was easy, Master Devereux, they just needed to give me a codeword, and I'd know where they'd come from, and the first pot of ale, a small one, mind you, was free," Master Tadwell said.

"Ah, I could see how that would work, and last night, how many times did customers come to your tavern and give you Merstake and Kidstowe's codeword?" Myles asked.

"Forty-three, sir. I was grateful; it made for a busy night again at the tavern," Master Tadwell said.

"You said 'again' – are we to assume that this had also happened on other nights?" Myles said, sounding shocked.

"Oh aye, sir, Merstake and Kidstowe have been sending men and women to the tavern for three nights. I'd already paid him ten farthings for his trouble," Master Tadwell provided.

"Ten! Good God!" Myles shot up from the stool. "That's ....." Myles made a show of calculating the number of people Merstake and Kidstowe had directed to the Thane's Arms. "He'd already sent a hundred people to your tavern, a hundred people, and we can assume these one hundred people had access to the brewery as well to see poor Master Garstang?"

"I don't know about that," Master Tadwell admitted.

"This is preposterous, I'm not listening to it anymore," Daytrew threw himself forward, his feet on the floor; he tried to rise from the low stool, but his legs failed to raise him, and he dropped back, the stool rattling noisily on the floor.

"Come now, Justice Daytrew, we've heard from Mistress Kent, Master Dodds, and now Master Tadwell, the landlord of the Thane's arms; surely you cannot discount all of their testimony?" Myles said, his voice reasoned.

"They'll no doubt say what they've been paid to say," Daytrew growled, trying again to force his legs to pull him back to the vertical.

"I would point out that Master Tadwell works not for me but for Garrison Bennett. Isn't that right, Master Tadwell?" Myles said.

Master Tadwell inclined his head in acceptance of the fact. "I do; indeed, Master Bennett owns the Thane's Arms."

"That must carry some weight, surely," Myles said, a note of feigned disappointment in his voice.

Grunting, Daytrew had almost succeeded in making it to his feet. Myles, with the agility of a greyhound, uncoiled himself and, grasping the Justice's arm, added his own weight to pull the man vertically. "Justice Daytrew, you are a hard man to convince."

"This is a concoction! I don't know why you've done this, but I intend to find out. When the Sheriff hears of this, it will not go well for you, sir," Daytrew said, huffing and rearranging his cloak around his shoulders.

"Very well then, let us take your men to the Sheriff. Have them place their complaint?" Myles said the sly note of confidence was not missed by Daytrew, who switched his gaze to where his men were still shivering by the fire. It didn't seem possible for them to pale even further, but they had.

"They don't look as if they would wish to, if I am honest, Justice Daytrew and I think I know why." Myles leaned towards Daytrew and said confidentially in his ear. "Not only were your men profiting from charging admittance to the brewery, they were also selling parts of the murdered man."

Daytrew's eyes widened, and his heavy chins pulled his slack mouth down.

"Master Dodds, if you would," Myles instructed.

Leggy strutted across the room towards his master, plumage rising around him. When he arrived, he produced a small purse, pulled the strings and with the practised skill of the showman, poured Garstang's teeth into the palm of his hand and presented them to Daytrew.

Daytrew, a look of disgust on his face, stepped backwards away from Leggy's raised hand.

"Exactly, distasteful are they not. Poor Master Garstang, deprived of life, then butchered and then being sold for a profit, it's not an enviable end, is it Master Daytrew?" Myles lamented, then examining the contents of Leggy's palm, he said, "there are four left; make a note of that, Peter; Master Garstang's head is bereft of teeth, and only four have been recovered. Your men, Justice Daytrew, have sold the rest."

The room was silent. No one moved. The bells of St Bride's struck and seemed overly loud as the noise rattled around the taproom. Myles waited until the last chime had run its course before speaking again. "I would make a guess that your men thought that the poor man had been butchered so badly that removing his teeth would not be noticed."

"Is this true," Daytrew's voice, high-pitched and filled with nerves squealed across the room towards his men cowering near the fire.

Their lack of response was confirmation enough.

"Dear Lord," Daytrew gasped.

"Precisely." Myles waved at Leggy, who retreated across the room. "Crinnion, sign the bottom of that sheet, then the lot of you, get out of here."

There was a sudden ripple of movement around the room. Daytrew's men were hauled back out, Mistress Kent and her daughter following. Crinnion rose, took the offered pen and quickly scratched his name before hurrying from the room. Tadwell followed, and Leggy Dodds sauntered out behind him. Soon, the only ones left in the room were Myles, Matthew and Justice Daytrew.

"Now, I believe the problem will be that there will be a coroner's inquisition. As tradition dictates, it will be held at the brewery, attended by the coroner, the sheriff and a jury he sees fit to appoint, and of course, at the centre of it all will be Master Garstang, or at least most of him. Your men did not do a very neat job of removing his teeth either; it will be obvious they are missing. Perhaps the coroner may assume they were taken by the murderer, given the state of the rest of the corpse; that is a very reasonable assumption. Unfortunately, there is a room full of witnesses here and a documentary record signed by the Parish Clerk, Crinnion, to attest to its authenticity, stating that poor Master Garstang was relieved of his teeth by your men."

Doubt, disbelief and distaste had been replaced on Daytrew's corpulent features with a look of horror.

Myles smiled. "I think we should turn our minds to finding a solution that is amenable to both of us, don't you?"

Shortly after Daytrew left, three of Master Drew's assistants were in the yard at the back of the White Hart. With them was a cart, and upon it boxes. Myles flipped a hessian cover back from one and grinned with delight when he found it filled with an assortment of hats and bonnets. Master Drew, it seemed, was about to make up for his poor choice of clients.

CHAPTER TWENTY

It was three days later when Myles accepted Tasker's invitation. Tasker's Inn, the Black Swan, was busy. The taproom was full, and many of the customers were seated under the eaves outside, backs against the wall, small squat, empty rundlet barrels providing seats.

Myles, Matthew slightly behind him, and followed by his usual retinue, entered the Inn.

Just inside the doorway to the right, a group of eight respectably dressed merchants were engaged in quiet and serious-looking discussions, on the table before them a document. Far too engaged with their own business, none looked up when Myles Devereux sauntered in, his men taking up what little space remained. Behind the merchants, three smiths, from the look of their bared arms and leather aprons, were seated near the fire. Before them, a platter of cooked goose, a woman wound her way by Devereux carrying three jugs of ale and heading towards them.

"Here ye go, my lads," she announced, setting down the ale between them.

To their right, a group of lawyers and a physician were seated around a table set with plates of steaming

Chance is a Game

food, and next to them, a dozen respectable-looking retainers were drinking and playing cards.

It was cramped, busy, and no doubt very profitable for Tasker.

Myles suppressed a bitter smile. Standing behind Tasker was his latest acquisition. Perkin, wrapped in soft velvet, primped and preened, was leaning beautifully against the end of the fireplace. Perkin's self-confidence was not as evident as it once had been; his tense pose and the quick, furtive glances towards Tasker were a testament to his fear. At the moment, he was evidently pleasing Tasker, and he was on show, a bauble to be admired, and from the look of him, he'd suffered no further beatings.

Perkin had been dressed to annoy. The doublet he wore was an almost perfect copy of a green one Devereux owned, the front ribbed with rows of silver buttons, the cuffs and collar trimmed with a lustrous emerald lace. It seemed there was to be no end to Tasker's impudence, but Myles was beyond annoyance tonight.

"I promised you a meal," Tasker said, sounding delighted, "and I shall not disappoint."

"Good, you have set the expectations high, Tasker," Myles replied, smiling broadly and following Tasker as he opened the door to the right of the fire that led to his private room. Perkin, behind Devereux, made a step towards the doorway.

"Out." Tasker waved his hand towards the boy, who froze on the threshold momentarily before managing to regain his composure and flounce back into the taproom.

Myles watched him go.

Tasker had noted Myles' gaze on the boy, as he was meant to, and he smiled broadly. "A wayward boy, sometimes."

"I've seen him somewhere before, I'm sure of it," Myles said, lowering himself into a chair at the table, his forehead creased with thought, "it will come to mind. I rarely forget a face."

It wasn't the reply Tasker had wanted. Perkin had been on display for Myles' benefit, Tasker said bluntly, "Indeed."

Myles rubbed his hands together in eager delight. "The smell from your kitchens, I can only hope, will be matched by what will be on the platters."

Tasker's sullen expression disappeared, and he smiled. "Simple fare, but well cooked, and I am sure you will enjoy it."

The meal was far from simple, and it was enjoyable. Pies, high-sided and steaming, filled with game and spices, were set on the table. There were roasted fowl, thick cuts of pork, pots of sweet, spiced conserve, fresh manchette bread, and a sugary fritter with almond custard. The latter particularly to Myles' taste.

Tasker smiled when Myles took a second wedge of the creamy dessert. "I knew you'd enjoy it."

"This." Myles tapped the plate, is a true delight. "Tasker, I am envious of your cook."

Tasker beamed happily. "Hospitality well provided is humbling."

Myles looked up suddenly from his meal, tapping the end of his knife on the table, and smiled. "The Angel, of course! Your boy was one of Nonny's lads. I knew I'd seen him before."

Tasker's face, which had been set into a fixed smile, dropped, the weight of his heavy jowls dragging his mouth into a dark scowl. "I don't think I recall seeing him there."

Myles pointed towards Tasker with the knife. "Yes, I do remember; he was lounging in the lap of one of my clients, Fitzwarren. You might have heard of him? He did invite me to join them, but I declined. I don't like to share my bedfellows. Could you pass the salt?"

Tasker automatically moved a hand towards the pot, an ugly cherub with a barrel containing fine white crystals on its back. He didn't pick it up but shoved it hard with his hand; it tipped, nearly toppling until Myles caught it, drawing it towards him.

"This pork is wonderful; I must ask where you got your cook? I might not want to poach the lad from your bed, but while you are not looking, I might become a thief in your kitchens," Myles said, laughing and skewering another slice of pork and delivering it to his plate.

Myles continued to enjoy the meal, complementing his host on the food, the wine, and the tableware. But knowing that Tasker was no longer listening, he was fuming over his comments about Perkin. His delicate and delightfully presented treasure had been likened to a gutter whore, shared already by the elite, turned down by his guest, and Tasker was furious. As he was meant to be.

Myles sat back and pushed the empty plate from him. He'd eaten far more than he had wanted to, but the mild discomfort his stomach was experiencing was nothing compared to the fury and rage that was running through the blood of the man opposite him.

Myles continued to not notice his host's loss of good humour and said. "I must return the compliment. The White Hart can, on occasion, provide good fayre. I cannot say for certain that it would equal what you have served tonight, but I shall have them try. Shall we say Saturday?"

"What?" Tasker replied; he'd stopped listening to Myles' constant meaningless compliments.

"I said, join me for a meal at the White Hart on Saturday," Myles repeated. "We have much to discuss. You've seen what your gold can buy, so it is time to conclude a deal."

That comment revived Tasker's attention; his pig-like eyes again fastened on his guest. "So, you are ready to sell?"

"I am, Tasker, I am," Myles said happily, "I can leave London a wealthy man, put behind me the stench of the city, the filth of its dealings. I might even find myself a wife. And thanks to you, this is possible. So, Saturday, Tasker and we can both get what we desire."

Perkin, attentive to Tasker's wishes, had been seated on a stool outside Tasker's room, and as soon as it opened, he sprang to his feet, draping himself artfully against the end of the fireplace.

Myles was closer now to the boy, and in the light from the lamp on the mantle, he could see beneath the powder a bruise swelling the line of his right cheekbone, the knuckles on his left hand were scraped of skin, and the final evidence of the abuse was a ring of bruises around his throat, a dark and patchy purple, partly obscured by the high collar of the doublet.

Myles met Perkin's eyes for a moment. Tasker, for a second, couldn't see the boy, and Perkin mouthed a silent plea towards Devereux.

"What did you say his name was, Tasker?" Myles suddenly said, stepping towards Perkin.

"I didn't," Tasker said from behind Myles.

"Definitely the same boy," Myles said, then to Perkin, "you remember Fitzwarren, don't you? I saw you with him at the Angel?"

Fear, bright as an anvil spark, flared in Perkin's eyes. This wasn't what he had wanted. The boy shook his head quickly.

"Yes, you do!" Myles said loudly, stepping towards the boy and giving his shoulder a playful punch. "I was betting with Nathaniel how many you'd take before your legs gave out."

Perkin untangled himself from the brickwork and stepped backwards, his face flour white and the scar from his eye to ear was now pronounced.

Myles turned to Tasker, laughing. "I lost four Angels that night."

Tasker's face was patched with rage, and Myles wasn't about to stop.

"I think Nathaniel only took the boy to make sure I lost," Myles said, reaching forward and clapping Perkin on the arm, "is that right, lad. Did you take Nat just to spite me?"

"Shut up!" It was Perkin's shrill voice; he made to dive past Myles towards the tavern door.

Tasker's fist hit him in the side of the head, and the boy staggered, his senses stunned, his arms reaching forward, trying to find something to grasp to steady himself.

Someone yelled. "Filthy whore!"

Another. "Stop him!"

An outstretched arm grabbed Perkin, hauling him into the embrace of the crowded Inn. The boy dragged suddenly, lost his balance and fell, howling, amongst a mass of arms, legs and fists. Perkin emerged above them once more, blood pouring down his face, his screams desperate.

Myles screwed his face up and stepped nearer to Tasker. "Well, I didn't think that would happen. Shall we say about seven on Saturday?"

A bloody, curdling scream rattled around the Inn, making Myles wince, and he threw a mild look of annoyance toward the affray.

"Stop them." Tasker had finally regained control of his voice; four of his men waded forward and began to batter the crowd away from Perkin. Now that serious injury could occur, the patrons fell back.

A small boy, fingers soiled with dirt, nails rimmed with black, disappeared beneath a table with the speed of a hunted hare. A swirl of rags and the sudden flash of two pale bare feet were all there was to see before the child had darted out of sight and back into the room's dark corners. Myles looked away quickly, his gaze returning to the wreckage of Perkin.

The boy, with blood dripping from his once fine face, lay still with his eyes closed. The rich doublet was ripped open; thieving hands had torn away the buttons, and blood, rose red, plumed on the linen of his shirt.

"I'm a physician, you animals, let me see the boy," a man seated with the merchants pushed through the crowd. His cap was askew, and he paused momentarily to set it right.

Myles rolled his eyes.

Chance is a Game

The physician dropped to his knees on the rushes next to Perkin, and the Black Swan Inn held its breath.

Raising his head, the long feathers on the hat catching around the shoulder clasp on his cloak and pulling his headwear sideways again. The physician announced formally. "The lad is dead."

There was a shuffling of feet away from the physician and Perkin. Any curiosity suddenly abandoned.

Myles stepped forward, his voice sharp as steel and an arm outstretched towards the onlookers. "You did this! Get him out of here, now!"

There was a moment where every man in the Inn stood stock still and stared at Devereux.

Myles broke it. "Now!" It was a command, and the inanimate patrons of a second ago dissolved into action. Perkin was blocked from view, surrounded by a dozen men, who then swiftly carried him from the tavern. He was followed by others; death was something no one wanted to be associated with, and the room silently emptied, food and ale cups abandoned on the tables.

Myles turned towards Tasker. "I apologise if these fools acted on my words. I blame myself. You've lost a night's trade, and your boy, I will recompense you for it. Saturday at seven, sir, and I can assure you that you will not be disappointed."

Before Tasker could reply, Devereux's own men had closed ranks around their master, and he was stepping towards the door, being careful to avoid the pond of blood on the floor.

CHAPTER TWENTY-ONE

Several tables and chairs for those attending deemed of sufficient standing to deserve one were brought into the brewery from the Bird Tavern. Master Garstang, naked and smelling less than fresh, was laid in lumps beneath hessian sacking, more to keep the flies away than to preserve him any dignity in death. Some thoughtful soul had placed a pot of rosemary on the end of the bench, but the competition from Garstang was too great; even the heavy aroma of the hops and ale couldn't be detected over the smell of the ripened remains.

Myles was present as Garstang's employer and the owner of the venue where the grizzly crime had been committed. In this capacity, if the death could be attributed to a fault in his employment, if Garstang had, for example, fallen through rotten planking, then the sheriff could levy exacting fines on Devereux. There was little chance of a fine in this case; it was murder, the jury would pronounce it as such, and the day was one of pure entertainment for Devereux.

Daytrew's discomfit, now he had the knowledge that some of the injuries to the corpse were attributable to his men, was apparent. Myles had attached himself to the justice and had the air of an excited child as they waited for the coroner, clerks, jury and sheriff to arrive.

Daytrew was provided with a chair, and Myles, as the owner of the brewery and because those carrying the chairs dare not do otherwise, also had one set for him next to the justice.

A physician, appointed by the coroner, had been there all morning, prodding and poking the remains, his youthful and serious assistant making notes as he was directed. Myles, his legs crossed, hands clasped around one knee, watched the spectacle with delight.

The physician's assistant abandoned his notes on the end of the table and, as instructed by his master, rolled over Garstang's pallid torso. The legs, cut away below the knee, were proving awkward obstacles for the young man. When he did finally turn the corpse over, he nearly succeeded in slithering it from the table.

The physician scowled at his assistant, who, blushing, retrieved his pen and paper. The older man, spectacles fixed on the end of a hooked and narrow nose, bent close to examine the back of the body. One of his fingers prodding the torn flesh just below a shoulder blade.

Myles leaned towards Daytrew. "He's found something of note on Garstang's back by the looks of it."

Daytrew didn't reply.

The physician made a quick request to his assistant, who handed him a short, smoothed, dowelled rod lined with markings. Pushing it into the hole on Garstang's back, he marked the dowel with a thumbnail, pulled it out and showed it to his assistant, who made a note.

"He's measuring the depth of the holes in his back," Myles replied unnecessarily as they watched the physician repeat the process on the opposite side of the corpse.

"All be upstanding." The sheriff's man, ahead of the procession of officials, announced from the doorway. Myles rose smoothly from his chair, enjoying the noises from Daytrew as he hefted his bulk to his feet. Chairs and benches from the Bird Tavern scraped on the brewery flags, a discordant trumpeting to announce the official's arrival. Myles caught the sheriff's eye as he entered and gave him a cold stare. The coroner was Thomas Cadwell, appointed by the Queen's Bench, and dressed against the cold of the occasion with a heavy fur-trimmed cloak and a bonnet similarly adorned. A serious expression on his face and trailed by two equally dour clerks. The jury, looking nervous, filed in, their eyes on the horrid remains in the centre of the cleared space.

There were a few moments of men moving to allow others access to the seats, a murmured uncurrent of 'thank you's' and 'excuse me's.' Then, another blast from the wood on the flags marked the end of the newcomers' arrival before silence settled on the brewery again.

One of the coroner's assistants rose, cleared his throat, and addressed those assembled. "The inquest into the death of Davyd Garstang of Lime Lane, an employee of Master Devereux and Brewer at the Tinwell brewery, is presided over by Coroner Thomas Cadwell. This session is declared a court of law under the jurisdiction of the Queen's Bench."

The physician paused his examination of the body when the officers and jury filed in.

"Pray continue, Master Drake," Cadwell said, waving a gloved hand towards the physician.

Drake returned to the table and spoke quietly to his assistant, the young man looking instantly unhappy with the instructions. It appeared he had been asked to turn the body back over. It involved a degree of rocking as the poor lad sought to gain the momentum he needed to heft the weight over. His cheeks were flushed as he tried to complete his task as quickly and efficiently as possible. His efforts jostled Garstang's innards, and the added pressure of the lad's arm on the enlarged stomach made the brewer produce one final loud fart as the torso settled onto its back.

Myles failed to contain a laugh, and he wasn't alone; amongst the jurors and officials, there was also the sound of poorly stifled laughter.

"May I remind those of you present that we might be in a brewery, but while I am here, this is a court of law, not an exhibition for your amusement," Cadwell admonished, addressing the physician. "Are you ready, Drake, to present your findings?"

Myles elbowed Daytrew. "Here we go."

Daytrew flushed.

"I am, your honour," Drake answered in a monotone voice. "Most of the damage to the body has been carried out post-mortem, but there is still evidence of the cause of the demise."

The physician waved his hand towards a pot on the floor, and his assistant placed it on the table and then raised Garstang's head, dropping the remains of the neck into the earthenware opening.

The physician turned the back of the head towards the Coroner and began to part the hair. "The bone is cleft away here, and the panicle that protects the brain has been wounded. It is my opinion that this blow would have rendered him unconscious, and the severity of it would have led to death."

"Can you determine the weapon that has been used?" Cadwell asked, leaning forward, his eyes on the back of Garstang's head.

The physician nodded, lifting a knife from his bag of tools he set to work on the back of Garstang's head. "The bone of the panicle has been broken along all four sides; it is held in place only by ...." He paused as he cut through hair and skin. ".... There we are; it's evident from the bone on the underside that this was a blow from a solid object rather than a blade; they tend to produce a chip or slice in the bone; this has, however, collapsed part of the skull."

"And your interpretation?" Cadwell asked his eyes on the piece of white bone with its shattered edges being held out for him to view.

It would have needed a significant blow, and I assume something like a hammer, the leverage of the shaft would be required to cause the damage. If I could remind you of the unfortunate case of Mistress Petty, who fell from the bridge and landed on one of the footing stones last year, this displays a similar level of damage."

The coroner nodded and rested back in his chair. "Is there anything else you can tell us?"

"The mutilation is post-mortem, as I said, and it has been undertaken with a degree of skill. The man who did it knew where to cut to avoid the bones, which would indicate to me he has done this before," the physician said, examining the cuts on the shoulder that had severed his arms. "Then there are the holes pierced in his back; the body was suspended on a double hook, a gambrel hook, I believe is the term, with one hook piercing the skin below each shoulder blade. It would have helped to stop the body turning away from the knife while he worked, again another indication he knew what he was about. The murderer's morbid fascination with his victim is seen as well; he has pulled his victim's teeth out, again post-mortem." The physician was handed a cloth by his assistant and began to wipe the blade he had used clean and then his hands.

"None were found?" The coroner sent the question towards Daytrew, where he sat next to Myles.

Daytrew shook his head; his cheeks were the colour of summer plums.

Myles couldn't resist rearranging himself on his seat, jabbing Daytrew in the side again, a gentle reminder.

"Hmmm, anything else?" The coroner returned his attention to the physician.

"A strong man, skilled with a knife, the killing blow probably from a hammer; there is not much else I can tell you; he's taken the teeth, I assume as some vulgar trophy of the event." The physician leaned towards Garstang's head and lifted the dark hair. "He also took his ears."

Myles' heart rang out so loudly he was sure those around him could have heard it. Missing ears could mean only one thing.

Daytrew stood to present his evidence, not that there was much of it. Myles distracted, wasn't listening, as Daytrew began his long-winded account of the chains, the vanishing man and their fruitless search of the docks, his mind was on Jeriah. Recent events would ensure that any mention Daytrew made of Devereux would only be in passing.

His suspicion that this was something to do with that evil cur, Jeriah, was fully confirmed; there could be no other reason for the brewer's ears to be missing.

Finch, he was sure, had gold he had obtained from Tasker. That could be the only leverage he could have had over Jeriah, it had to be greed that had saved him. Whether there was still a connection with Garrison Bennett, he did not know.

CHAPTER TWENTY-TWO

The outer room at the White Hart, where Devereux's debtors presented themselves, had been transformed into a lavish dining room. Unlike Tasker's, the tableware was Italian, matched, and was of the current fashion. A side table held wine and delicate Venetian glasses.

Devereux held the door open for Tasker. "Please, take a seat. I shall serve you myself. Tonight's words are not ones either of us would wish to be overheard."

Tasker, smiling, lowered his bulk into the offered chair, and Myles, turning towards the wine glasses, winced as he heard the wooden frame creak in complaint, but, as a testament to a good carpenter, the chair held and when he turned to present Tasker with wine, he was still seated and had not been delivered to the floor.

"Try this, it is exquisite. I have had some brought from Spain, a new variety called Malvasier." Myles poured wine into two delicate Venetian glasses.

Tasker took the offered glass; Myles raised his to his lips, and Tasker did the same. "Sweet and as thick as honey."

Tasker smiled. "You are right. That is delicious."

Myles, looking pleased, set his glass down. "I thought you'd like it. Once the deal is finalised, I shall have some sent over to you."

Tasker put his glass down on the table, and, raising his eyes from it, said seriously, "business is after all why I am here."

Myles smiled and wagged a finger at Tasker. "Business is only one reason, first we eat. I promised you a meal, and I hope the White Heart will not disappoint."

Tasker was, Myles found, easily diverted. Anyone who had taken the time to build himself a body like Tasker's was a man who enjoyed food. As a monk, he would have enjoyed the very best the local land had to offer, and Tasker was happily sending mouthful after mouthful to his vast stomach. Meanwhile, Myles kept up a one-sided conversation about the food, London, the weather and the Privy Council's latest laws that were attempting to curb his profits. Myles knew that Tasker was giving almost all his attention to the food, but he didn't care. He topped up his guest's glass five more times during the meal, but not his own.

The final dish was an apple and quince pie, beautifully decorated, sweet and aromatic. It wasn't to Myles' taste, and he'd pushed the confection around the plate, waiting for Tasker to consume his. Myles preferred a bitter edge to his fruit; it reminded him of what it was; the pudding before him was purely cast of sugar and designed only to impress. To Myles, it was cloying, false and gave him a headache, not that he would ever say so, that would have been against the current fashion. While Myles waited for Tasker to finish, his mind wandered to the subject of sugar. It wasn't something he had ever been involved with; perhaps he should. It was hugely profitable, although

Chance is a Game

he knew from other merchants' experience that it could also be ruinous. Sugar was a cargo that was easily spoilt or lost, and Myles liked to avoid risking too much. Risk was necessary, a part of the game of life, but like a cat, Myles possessed a sixth sense of when it was time to stop pushing his luck.

Like a cat!

Myles abandoned his spoon noisily on the plate, the sweetness of the sugar in his mouth suddenly more unpleasant.

Looking across the table at Tasker, it took a moment to replace the smile that had suddenly fallen from his face. It needn't have mattered; the monk was giving his full attention to his food. Myles forced himself not to sour his expression when Tasker began raking his spoon across the plate to gather the last sweet juice from the dessert. Idly, he wondered if he'd raise the plate to his meaty lips and clean the last of it dog-like.

Myles was, on that score, disappointed.

Tasker discarded his spoon on the table, wiped his hand across his mouth and sat back, the carpenter's pegged joints creaking in further annoyance. "I'll give you that, Devereux, it was better than my kitchen can produce, but I still think my boar was superior."

Myles smiled, rising as he refilled Tasker's glass. "A point each, very good."

"So, to business?" Tasker asked, picking his glass up.

"Why not. You've seen what I have to offer; you have gauged the extent of it, and I am sure that you can see that it is worth the price I placed upon it," Myles said, settling back in the chair, his legs crossed, his hands resting loosely in his lap.

Tasker's fat fingers wrapped around the delicate stem of the glass, twisting it, his eyes for a moment breaking from Myles' gaze and fastening instead on his empty plate. "There are now other matters that need to be taken into account. The loss of the Unicorn and the murder of Garstang will impact your business. There will be costs involved to pay out, and of course, you will have lost a great deal of business. You cannot, at the moment, continue to supply ale to the city's taverns so that business is lost to you, and you have to buy in ale for your own taverns, so your profit will be lowered."

Myles tipped his head to one side and regarded Tasker with a level gaze. "You do make fair points. However, the loss of the Unicorn has made way for a phoenix-like resurrection, but on a grander scheme, and likewise with the brewery it will rise again with increased capacity."

Tasker smiled; his tone was sympathetic when he spoke. "I am sure they will, but this will take time and of course, money. I need to factor this in when I am making this offer."

"Go on," Myles prompted, not sounding annoyed at all.

"You asked for a thousand pounds. I would be happy to give you four hundred, which is a very fair price, and I will take over rebuilding both of those businesses; it's a good offer, Myles, and I am sure you know it. London is not the haven for you it once was, and this would provide you with plenty of gold to take wherever you wish," Tasker finished; now he had stated his case, his confidence had returned, and his eyes met those of Myles once more.

Myles folded his arms and looked thoughtful; it was a moment before he spoke. "I can understand your concerns, Tasker, but your price is slightly low. It will not cost a fraction of that to rebuild the Unicorn or improve the brewery."

"Myles, it is not as simple as just the reconstruction costs. I was a prior and a treasurer for my order, and I understand how these things will impact in the longer term. It will take a year to rebuild the Unicorn; even if you start now, it will take time for men's habits to change. They will have found other taverns to use other places to buy food. At the very least, it will take another two years to get the income back to the level you had before the fire. The same is true with the brewery; men must buy ale for their taverns, and deals will have been struck elsewhere. Overcoming those will take a long time, and I doubt that the brewery will ever sell as much as it used to. That business has been lost to you," Tasker said, his tone sorrowful.

"I have one last thing I wanted to show you myself; I honestly feel that when you view it, you will want to revise your offer. Believe me, you will like it," Myles said, his voice pleasant.

Smiling, Myles rose from his chair, and with effort, Tasker did the same, using the table's edge to lever himself upright. Before he followed Myles towards the door, he picked up the fine Venetian glass and drained it.

Myles smiled.

Holding the door open for Tasker, he began another monologue as they descended the stairs.

In the taproom of the White Hart were several patrons, and a more significant number of Tasker's men were scattered among them. Seeing their master following Myles Devereux down the stairs, they all stood, making their presence obvious. Some of Myle's men were among them, but in lesser number.

Myles continued to talk as he descended the stairs. "It's just behind the tavern, a few moments of your time you will not regret spending."

Myles rounded the bottom of the stairs, and underneath them was a door, one of Myles' men opened it. Tasker's men moved across the tavern closer to their master.

"It's a small room, and you'll want to see this on your own," Myles said, stepping inside.

Tasker waved a hand towards his men, who remained in the White Hart's taproom. Following Myles inside, the door closed behind him.

There was nothing in the room apart from a small table in the centre, over which was draped a rich blue velvet cloth. Tasker looked at Myles in confusion.

Myles smiled and whipped the cloth from the table. The gold of the astrologica glittered in the candlelight. Myles wore a pleased expression, his eyes fixed on the intricate mechanism. "It is truly wonderful."

Tasker stepped towards the table. "What is it?"

"I was, like you, confused. I'd never seen it's like before. But let me show you," Myles said with the enthusiasm of a happy child.

From around his neck, he retrieved a delicate chain; at the end was the small key that fitted into the astrologica.

"This is the key." Myles held it up reverently. "If you come around to this side, you will be able to observe the mechanism better."

Tasker moved around to the opposite side of the table where Myles had pointed and watched as the key was inserted, and Myles began to wind it slowly. "It is a matter of some care; it has to be wound fully but not overwound. The box issues a loud click when it has reached that point."

Myles continued to turn the key, listening intently. Tasker, too, his head on one side was listening.

"A little further, I think," Myles said.

There was a sudden click audible in the room. Myles smiled, and so did Tasker.

"When were you born?" Myles asked suddenly.

Tasker looked confused.

"I have no evil intent, sir. This has been the key to my success, and when I show you how it works, you will have a much better understanding of the worth of my business. The date, please."

"August 14th," Tasker said quietly, licking his lips.

Myles looked up from the device and met Tasker's eyes. "Leo, a fine sign. Ferocious, competent and intelligent. I should have known."

Tasker smiled.

"So, we place this wheel here to set the date, and then we press this ...." Myles said, his voice quiet; he lay a finger on the golden lever, his eyes meeting Tasker's, ".... now we wait."

Tasker, engrossed by the turning golden wheels, watched until, with a final quiet click, they stopped.

"Now what," Tasker's voice was a whisper in the room.

"We read your horoscope," Myles said, approaching the box. His hands planted on either side of the golden automata as he studied the top.

"What does it say?" Tasker said, breaking the silence.

Myles raised his gaze from the box, and his dark, cold eyes met with Tasker's. "That's strange. It's telling me the same as when I had my own recently cast.

"What?" Tasker pressed; his voice urgent.

Myles' tone changed. It was cold, hard and business-like. "I see a short life, brought to an end by incaution and arrogance, and I would add to that avarice."

Tasker's eyes snapped up from the box to Myles' face.

Myles, a knife in his hand, observed him coolly over the table. "You are drunk, Tasker. There is incaution. You've had wine sweetened with mead to hide the tang of the aqua vitae, and if that was not enough, the gravies and sauces you practically licked from my dishes were drenched in more."

"I'm not drunk," Tasker barked, anger beginning to flush his cheeks.

"Oh, you are, and it's made you incautious. Why else would you be foolish enough to have entered this room alone," Myles replied.

"My men are outside. I have more than you here. Do you think I'd be foolish enough to walk into the middle of your web without an army at my back," Tasker spat back, stepping towards the door.

"By all means, open the door, call them," Myles invited lightly.

Tasker's plump hand fastened on the door handle, and he hauled it open, his eyes roving the taproom on the other side. There were no longer any patrons seated drinking and eating; his own men were gone, and instead the room was filled with Devereux's men, armed and all staring at him.

Tasker flung the door shut.

"So incautious, as I said. This brings us to my other prediction: arrogance. A sin if I am correct. I would have thought your monks' training would have helped you avoid the trap, but apparently not," Myles said, his voice amused.

Tasker didn't reply.

Myles sighed. "How dare you think you could make such an offer for my business and believe I would settle for worthless church trinkets? Arrogance led you to believe I am a fool, and I don't believe I am. But as they say, business is a game, and chance is a game as well, and you played chance with your life Tasker. High stakes."

"What are you saying?" Tasker growled.

"I will allow you the arrogance of making a derisory offer for my business that does me no harm. Indeed, it was amusing. However, burning down the Unicorn and ruining my brewery were a step too far. For those, I wish recompense, and I'll take your church trinkets and call it even. That deal would have been on the table, and you could have left here unharmed. But you went a little too far," Myles' voice grated angrily.

"Don't think I kept that gold at the Black Swan; it's away from there, and I'm the only man who knows. You'll not find it?" Tasker growled.

Myles turned the knife in his hand, a sad expression settling on his face. "I'm afraid that's not true. I do know where it is. Indeed, should you go to the location where you believe it is secure, you'll find it has already gone. Myles leaned below and pulled out a gold chalice, which had been hidden by the velvet draped over the table.

Tasker's eyes blazed with fury.

"As I was saying before you interrupted …."

"How did you find it?" Tasker growled.

"Well, that brings us back to arrogance and incaution, a terrible mixture of both in your case. Perkin told me," Myles said levelly, forcing himself to keep a tone of triumph from his voice.

"Perkin? He's dead!" Tasker threw back.

"Yes, well, perhaps. But before Perkin was beaten in your tavern, you liked to fuck him on top of your golden treasures. Can't have been comfortable for the lad, but I don't think you ever had much concern for Perkin, did you?" Myles replied coolly.

"The traitorous, little shit," Tasker cursed.

"Precisely, and a product of your own actions. Your lack of care for Perkin has been, I am afraid, your undoing." Myles summarised. "But we digress; as I was trying to say, I would have taken your stolen gold and sent you from here with your tail between your legs, the price for incaution and arrogance. However, you went further than destroying the brewery and the Unicorn, didn't you?"

Tasker, for a moment, looked confused. "What are you talking about."

"It's quite simple. Answer me one question, truthfully and immediately, or I shall leave you to your fate that waits on the other side of that door," Myles' voice was cold.

"What bloody question?" Tasker said.

There was a pause, the room filled with the silence of expectation.

"*WHERE TASKER, IS MY CAT?*" Myles' voice was loud, and Tasker jumped backwards. Anyone standing beyond the door would have heard the question.

"Your what? Cat?" Tasker blurted.

Myles glared at him. "If I was you, I would answer the question. That alone might save you."

"I don't know anything about a damned cat," Tasker said.

Myles exhaled loudly and said, "last chance, Tasker."

Tasker looked wildly about the room, searching for an escape, a weapon, anything.

"Matthew," Myles shouted.

The door opened, it wasn't Matthew who was standing there staring into the interior, the candlelight highlighting the thin scar that ran from eye to ear. It was Perkin.

Myles held up the knife. "He is all yours."

"How? He's dead!" Tasker gawped at Perkin.

"Patently not," Myles said; about to turn and leave, he stopped himself, vanity the victor. "The Unicorn fell, and then you poisoned my ale, and you were foolish enough to believe that all your new patrons were arriving because of this. You were profiting from my loss; I would lay a wager that you revelled in it. Can you remember some of your new customers? A group of smiths, perhaps? Some lawyers, a physician and a group of well-dressed, if not overly convincing, merchants – which reminds me I have yet to take my men to task for their poor performance. Percy pretending to be a physician while drunk was unforgivable, and I thought it would give the game away."

Tasker gawped at him. "Your men?"

Myles smiled. "Over half of your taproom was full of my men, listening, watching, and they were there to fall on Perkin, rip master Drew's creation to shreds and pour pigs blood over him. And if I recall, I do think they rather overdid that. I think it is unlikely any of them will be making a career on the stage."

"So, he wasn't even injured?" Tasker said, confused.

"Keep up. Tasker. You've been duped. No, he's not dead, or injured, or even slightly bruised. He's here and beautifully filled with vengeance and anger, aimed primarily towards yourself," Myles said, smiling.

Two men suddenly pressed by Perkin, and for a fleeting moment, Tasker's eyes lit with a hope that was quickly extinguished when they grasped his arms and pinioned him against the wall.

Myles held the knife out for Perkin to take. "Well, it has been a pleasant evening. I shall leave you two together."

"Wait, wait ...." Tasker practically screamed. "Finch, Bennett's man, set your tavern on fire."

Perkin had relieved Myles of the knife, the lamplight flitting along the sharpened blade. Myles' face clouded with annoyance. "Finch told me he was selling my beer to Garrison Bennett, and you knew just how much that would infuriate me. However, Bennett wasn't too pleased when he found out you'd been using his name. And if that was not enough, your monkish friends allowed you access to Clerkenwell Priory to the powder that was being stored there. I am sure when you found you could lay your hands on that, it was just a matter of planning how you could use it to your best advantage."

Tasker just gawped at Myles.

"Chance is a game, Tasker, and you are out of rolls of the dice," Myles said, stepping from the room.

Matthew closed the door as soon as Myles was back inside the tavern, and two of his men took up a guard on the door.

Myles, his head suddenly throbbing, began to make his way up the stairs. He was halfway up when he heard the first scream. Christ! All this planning, and he'd overlooked the fact that the room Tasker and Perkin were in was beneath his own. He hoped the racket wasn't going to go on all night. Resignedly, he continued up the stairs. The monk certainly had a good pair of lungs, probably all those years of chanting.

Myles opened the door at the top of the stairs and stepped inside. It still smelt of the sickly meal he had served for Tasker; most of the dishes were now gone, and Susie, a cloth in her hand, was wiping wine and food stains from the table. She paused and smiled when he entered the room.

A scream followed by a sob wound its way through the floorboards. Both of them ignored it.

"Susie, if it is not too late, could you bring me some food?" Myles asked.

"After that meal you had tonight!" Susie said, sounding shocked.

"I didn't eat very much," Myles said simply, picking up the last of the spiked wine he held the bottle towards her. "Take this away as well."

"What would you like?" Susie asked, taking the bottle.

"Something simple. Bread, cheese, ham and ale," Myles replied, heading towards the door to his room.

Opening the door was a relief. The air inside wasn't tainted with the sickly smell of the meal, and the sounds from below were muffled. Slowly, Myles unbuttoned his doublet, and pulling it off, he draped it over a chair back. The shutters were open and showed a night sky pricked with stars. Myles was about to drop into one of the chairs by the fire when he heard a noise from his bed.

Turning, his eyes locked with the yellow ones of Amica. Arranged on his pillow, the cat mewed a second time.

"You did that on purpose," Myles said, scooping the cat from the bed and reclining in the chair with Amica in his lap.

Sam Burnell

CHAPTER TWENTY-THREE

There was a light tap on the door. Food was waiting for Myles in the other room. Putting an annoyed Amica on the floor, he opened the door to find a laden tray on the table, and Susie was about to open the outer door and leave.

"Stay a moment," Myles pulled a chair from the table and, sitting down, pulled the tray towards him.

Susie walked back and stood at the end of the table. "Bread's not the freshest; it's this mornings, sorry."

"Sit down," Myles waved a hand towards the chair Tasker had been seated in not long ago.

Susie drew the chair out, the legs scraping on the floor.

"How much do you think I can eat?" Myles said, pointing to the mountain of food on the tray. "Help yourself."

Susie hesitated.

"Go on ...." Myles encouraged.

Susie took a slice of bread and rolled a piece of ham up, then pressed a knife through the soft, crumbling yellow cheese, taking from the end a neat, fine sliver.

"For God's sake, woman, take some more." Myles quickly cut two more pieces, dropped them on her platter, spiked another two slices of ham, and deposited them on top.

The colour had risen to Susie's cheeks, and her eyes were on the food before her.

The outer door leading to the stairs suddenly opened. It was Matthew. His quick eyes took in the scene in the room, and a look of obvious disapproval creased his face.

"What?" Myles said, annoyed at the intrusion.

"Perkin wants to see you," Matthew said, his cold gaze on Susie, making her look away.

"Does he, indeed," Myles replied. "As you can see, I'm busy. Tell him to come back tomorrow."

"Is that wise?" Matthew said, "he needs to know his place, or there'll be trouble."

"More than there has already been tonight?" Myles said, one eyebrow raised.

"You know what I mean," Matthew said, "see him. Put him in his place."

Myles exhaled loudly. "If I must. Make him wait an hour."

Matthew nodded, cast a final displeased glance in Susie's direction, and left.

Myles continued to eat, and Susie picked at her plate.

"You are hardly good company, are you?" Myles complained, slopping ale from the jug into two of the cups and then sliding one towards Susie. "Tell me something."

Susie shrugged. "Like what?"

"I don't know anything," Myles said, tearing the end from a loaf of bread.

Still, Susie remained nervously silent.

"God, when we were soaked to our skins in that alley, you had enough to say for yourself. What's the

Chance is a Game

difference now?" Myles said, a note of annoyance in his voice.

Susie shrugged again. "I dunno."

"Well, try," Myles said.

"You weren't Myles Devereux then," Susie replied quietly.

"That's a start. Anything else?" Myles continued between mouthfuls.

"I don't want to get into trouble," Susie said.

There was a sudden banging noise from below, followed by what sounded like a bulky object being dragged across the floor.

"Is he dead?" Susie asked suddenly.

"Tasker? I don't know," Myles replied, cutting more cheese from one of the blocks on the tray. "Have some of this one. I can recommend it."

There was another loud bang from below, and someone cursed. Susie jumped.

Myles sighed and put down his knife. "Do not have any fear; whatever happened to Tasker isn't going to happen to you. And Tasker's demise or injury wasn't at my hands."

Susie looked up. "I know, and I can't blame the lad, either. Master Tasker were a vicious cur."

A sudden guttural moan leaked up through the floorboards to them.

Myles grinned. "I think you might need to change your tense; Tasker sounds like he's still with us."

Susie smirked. Then, horrified, she slapped a hand to her mouth to cover her smile.

Myles laughed, then pointing towards her with the knife, he asked, "Perkin, you've got to know him over the last few days while he's been here. What do you think of him?"

"I feel sorry for him; he's had a rough time of it at that man's hands," Susie replied.

"I've saved him from Tasker. Do you think he values that?" Myles asked, watching Susie closely.

The woman shook her head.

Myles stabbed a piece of pie viciously. "Why doesn't that surprise me. Doubtless, he chooses to believe I placed him in harm's way?"

The look on Susie's face was answer enough.

"Inspired loyalty is very different to the paid equivalent," Myles observed dryly.

Susie looked confused. "Why, I don't understand?"

Myles smiled wryly. "If it's paid for, then you can be outbid, something Tasker recently found out when he lost the support of his men tonight. The promise of better pay, cemented with free food and ale, was enough to change their allegiance."

Susie nodded. "That's a fair point."

"I can't inspire loyalty, so I buy it, as I will have to do with Perkin. A man I know can, but it's an ability I seem to lack," Myles mused.

"Is he a friend?" Susie asked.

Myles' brow furrowed. Was he? Was Fitzwarren a friend? It wasn't something he'd ever considered before. He'd undoubtedly been his brother's friend. "I'm not sure."

"Well, then ask yerself another question, are you loyal to him?" Susie said.

Myles laughed. "Loyal to Fitzwarren ..." Then he stopped himself. Maybe he was! Maybe that damned man had, over the years, gained his loyalty without trading a single silver coin, and Myles had never noticed.

"So, you do have a friend," Susie smiled.

"You ...." Myles said, pointing towards the woman with the knife again, "are beginning to remind me of my mother! Always right, although I'd never admit it."

Susie smiled, her face sad. "Well, it's been a long time since I 'ad a son. But the Lord knows I am still a mother."

"I'm sorry, it wasn't my intention to sour your mood," Myles said.

"It's alright," Susie replied, her eyes on the food before her.

Myles tried to think of something to say; realising the silence was becoming overly long, he asked, "your son, tell me what happened to him?"

"Ma boy?" Susie said, "Why?"

"I'm interested, that was all," Myles said, feeling awkward that he'd asked the wrong question and waved the knife towards her in encouragement.

"There's not much to say; he just disappeared. Went wi' ma husband to work and didn't come back. Ma husband worked with the chippy's at North Lane, and Thomas at the mill. He just disappeared, and then when ma husband went looking for him he didn't return either," Susie said.

"Both of them? What happened?" Myles said, his natural cat-like curiosity taking hold.

"I don't know, no one does," Susie said.

"Come on, a man and child can't just go missing without someone knowing where they went or what happened?" Myles said, an edge of disbelief creeping into his voice.

"I were blamed, for driving ma husband, Thomas away, and that's wa' people said, that it was ma fault. He'd gone an' taken the boy with 'im," Susie said.

Myles considered this for a moment, the end of the knife tapping the table. "Did you argue? Women aren't always in accord with their husbands."

Susie exploded from the chair, the platter before her caught on the edge of her dress and emptied onto the table. "Thomas Herrington were a good man, and he loved me. He'd not 'ave left me and taken my boy, John, with him."

"I was just …." Myles tried, but it was pointless; his company for the evening had already stormed from the room.

Bloody women! You never knew what was happening inside their heads. He'd tried, and look where that had got him? Myles pulled the tray towards himself, turned it so the thick ham slices were closer and helped himself to two more; then, with his knife, he cut a careful piece of cheese and reduced it to small, neat cubes for Amica.

At least you knew where you were with a cat. Feed it, and you retain its affection. It was a little like loyalty. He was sure he would lose his cat if someone had a larger piece of cheese. The type of loyalty Fitzwarren dealt in he didn't understand.

Myles put Amica back on the bed, whipped the doublet from the chairback, slid his arms in and began to fasten the buttons. By the time he had finished, he could hear the sound of footsteps on the stairs.

Myles smoothed down a crease in the fabric on his right sleeve and opened the door.

"Perkin to see you, Master," Matthew announced as soon as he entered the room.

"A private conversation, Matthew." Myles waved a hand at Matthew, who immediately retreated, closing the door to the stairs. He would, Myles knew, be on the other side.

Myles folded his arms and regarded Perkin with a direct, cold stare. "Well? What do you want?"

It was certainly not the welcome Perkin expected, and uncertainty cracked his mask of arrogance for a second. "I thought you would want to thank me."

Myles laughed. "For what?"

"I have helped you get rid of Tathker," Perkin replied. "We had a bargain. I get th' Black Thwan."

Myles shook his head. "When, exactly, did I say that?"

Perkin's eyes narrowed. "You told me you would put me in Tathker's plath if I helped you."

Myles found the edge of the desk and leaned against it. "That's maybe what you heard, but that's not actually what I said."

"What do you mean?" Perkin's anger started rising.

"I said that if you helped me, then I would put you in charge of the Black Swan. That's very different," Myles said.

"I don't get the tavern?" Perkin stammered.

"No. You work for me. The Black Swan is mine, and you, with help, can appear as its owner," Myles said.

"The bargain was the tavern, and I'll not leave with less, you've had Tathker murdered. Do you want that fact known abroad?" Perkin spat.

"Well, that at least answers a question," Myles dropped from the desk, uncoiled like a snake, and struck his hand around the boy's throat. Hearing the noise, Matthew opened the door, not at all happy about leaving his master in the same room as the murderous Perkin.

"Let us consider the facts," Myles hissed into the boy's face. "Forty men just saw you take a knife and enter a room with Tasker. Forty. Who, exactly, is going to disbelieve the testimony of forty men? And as yet, you've not even taken the time to wash the blood from the backs of your hands. You had good reason to kill him; you've complained enough about it during the last few days while you've been here. Now, tell me again, what are you threatening me with?"

Perkin was white.

Myles pushed him backwards.

"Matthew, return him to the Black Swan, find a water trough on the way to douse him in, and introduce him to the men who will be ensuring he acts only in my interests," Myles said, then looking back at Perkin, "do we understand each other? It is more than a good bargain; you will appear as the new landlord of the Black Swan. Tasker's body will be found, and men will wonder what happened, and tongues will rattle, and tales will be told. But they will be tales. I hold the proof. So, take what you have been given and enjoy it."

Perkin nodded. "Yeth." His voice was high pitched and trembling.

"Yes, what?" Matthew said, a fist clamping painfully on the boy's arm.

"Ahhh .... Mathter Devereux .... Yeth Mathter Devereux .... Ahhh," Perkin shouted.

"Let him go, Matthew," Myles' voice was pleasant again. "I would, as it happens, have been unhappy had you not challenged me. All men need to know their place. And now you know yours. Stay in it, Perkin, and we will all step happily along the road to heaven. Stray from it, and there will be a rope around your neck next time."

Matthew took charge, taking Perkin from the room. A push in the small of his back sent him stumbling towards the door.

Myles watched them go.

Finally, the day was done.

When he returned to his room, he found Amica had moved from the bed to his chair by the fire. Scooping her up, he sat down and rested back, eyes closed. His long ringed fingers smoothed down the black fur, and the cat purred with delight when his hand opened and revealed the cubes of cheese.

Myles, his eyes closed, smiled.

CHAPTER TWENTY-FOUR

Two weeks later

Myles, followed by four of his men, walked through the busy taproom of the White Hart. A loud cheer erupted from a corner of the room as he did. Myles turned to look. A man was fishing in the bottom of his ale cup and held up a dripping coin a moment later, whooping as he did.

Myles smiled and continued towards the stairs. His ale was selling, his taverns will full, probably more so than before Garstang had been thrown into the brewing vats.

Matthew had told him his scheme was ridiculous but had conceded to try it. One of Matthew's more reliable men was posted at each of his taverns, in charge of a small purse of coins. At night, these were dropped into ale cups, unknown to the customers. Mainly farthings, but there was the odd groat and a few pennies to be found, and at the White Hart, even a silver shilling had emerged from the bottom of an ale cup. News like this travelled fast, and the taverns were full.

Matthew dropped into step next to him. "I'll give you this one. You were right."

"Thank you, Matthew," Myles said, a satisfied tone in his voice. "The cost of those few lost coins is nothing compared to the profit."

"I know, and the taverns are full. At the Bird in Hand, they serve ale outside in the rain, and there's no space left inside. It's brought men back, but will they stay once you stop salting the beer with coins?" Matthew said.

"We'll do this for a few weeks; by then, men will be used to where they are drinking, will have made associations, and found where they like to sit. There is nothing quite as reliable as a comfortable habit, Matthew, and that is what we are working to produce," Myles said, looking pleased.

His other instructions had been followed as well. The two fires in the White Hart were blazing, spreading welcome heat around the room, and winding between the tables was Susie, a basket on her hip, and inside it a dozen loaves of bread cut into chunks, hers to give to whoever she chose.

A warm welcome, free food and the chance to leave a wealthier man. Myles Devereux's taverns were back in business.

It wasn't only coins found in Devereux's taverns that week either. Matthew tipped the wooden cup's contents into the palm of his gloved hand and smiled. Raising his eyes, he met Rogan's pleased expression. "I'll keep this and take the rest to Finnell. And this." Matthew transferred the pearl to his purse and fished out a silver coin. "Is for you."

Rogan's eyes sparkled with delight.

Myles wasn't sure what woke him, the cold, a draught in the air, Amica sliding from his lap. Whatever it was, it was just in time; his eyes opened, and they should have been looking at the open window and the dark silhouette of St Brides.

But the view was gone.

Blocked by the outline of a man.

Myles was out of the chair, darting away from the trap near the fire, bare feet bringing him to the end of the bed. A candle, wavering in the draft from his movement, sent a pale light across the face of Jeriah, who leered at him.

Christ!

"That's a fine-looking bed," Jeriah said, licking his lips.

Myles' left hand was resting on the carved end-post.

Time. Time.

"I'll not ask how you got in, or who is dead," Myles' hand slowly lowered itself down the carving on the bedpost.

Jeriah uttered a delighted wheezing laugh. Lifting a cord from around his neck, he brandished it towards Myles. The two most recent ears that had been added to the revolting jewellery were bloodied and pale. "They never hear Jeriah. No one ever hears poor Jeriah."

Myles' hand moved slowly down over, his fingertips caressing the carpenters, chiselled unseen relief on their descent.

Jeriah released his bloody trinkets and took a lumbering step forward.

"Tell me, Jeriah, where's Finch?" Myles said quickly. His hand had left the wood and, for a moment, found only the empty air behind the post.

Jeriah raised a finger and wagged it at Myles. "You'll not trick me. Jeriah's no fool."

The big man took two more heavy steps forwards. Myles' hand found the sword's hilt at the same moment. Leaping backwards, he kept the distance between them, his left hand ripping the scabbard from the blade.

The flame, disturbed for a second time, sent a flickering glimmer along the blade's sharp edge.

"Back off, Jeriah," Myles growled, knowing full well the other man wouldn't.

Jeriah hefted the hammer in his hand.

There was one chance.

Just one.

If Jeriah closed the gap, he'd be lost. A second of doubt clouded his face, and Myles saw it reflected in Jeriah's malevolent grin as the big man lurched forwards.

From behind Jeriah came a rattle, followed by a click and a whirr. The alien noise stole the goaler's attention, his head turning towards the sound.

Myles, his full weight behind the sword, lunged forward, praying he had the strength to force it through the leather-clad chest and that beneath it was nothing more than linen and flesh.

The sword point hit his target, slowed, and then stopped. Myles threw himself against the hilt and felt the resistance thankfully give as the steel slid through Jeriah's ribs.

Matthew, flinging open the door, arrived just in time to witness the look of shocked disbelief on Jeriah's face before it, and his body crumpled. Behind Jeriah, on the desk, Amica, hissing, stood with her paws on the Astrologica.

Want More?

A TIME TO DECIEVE – Is the next Myles Devereux Mystery

OR

Follow the adventures of Richard Fitzwarren in the

Mercenary For Hire Series

By Sam Burnell

If you enjoyed this book why not help other readers out and share your thoughts with them so they can find a good historical fiction read.

Sam Burnell

The End

Printed in Great Britain
by Amazon